P9-BBT-605

INCIDENT AT PISHKIN CREEK

Also by Gary D. Svee

SPIRIT WOLF

CHAPTER 1

MAX Bass stood on the boardwalk, stiff as the starched shirt he wore. His shirt was scratchy, hot, and too tight around the collar, not that a man could breathe in this abominable heat, anyway. But worse, the shirt was a lie, part of a costume Max was wearing to make a lie more believable—to make himself a more believable liar.

Damn shirt!

Max felt like a forgotten soldier on a drill field standing at attention, waiting for someone to tell him "at ease." But no one did, so he stood uneasy, shoulders squared and a wilted bouquet of prairie flowers held across his chest in a liar's salute.

Only his eyes moved, mostly to the southeast, watching for the puff of dust that would indicate the stage was coming from Ingomar. She would be coming that way: train from Boston to Montana and then stagecoach from Ingomar to Prairie Rose.

Max ran a finger between the stiff collar and his neck. If he were a sweating man, he'd be drenched now, but Montana summers had dried the sweat out of him long ago.

Damn heat!

A little breeze would give a man some relief, but there was none, not even a flicker among the leaves of the cottonwoods that lined the creek on the edge of town. Still Max knew it wasn't the heat that was preying on his mind: It was waiting for his bride-to-be, a woman he had not yet met.

Damn shirt!

He should have worn his usual gear, a rough pair of pants and a long-sleeved flannel shirt. This stiff collar was a lie, just like the lie he had put in the Boston newspaper:

> *Montana rancher and coal mine owner seeking younger woman with matrimony object of intentions. Interested parties may write Max Bass, General Delivery, Prairie Rose, Montana.*

Max wasn't accustomed to lying. But he had lied to Catherine O'Dowd because she wouldn't have come if he had told her the truth. Likely no woman would have, no woman Max would want anyway.

The lie ran on long after Miss O'Dowd and a dozen other women had answered his advertisement. Max studied each of the letters for hours, seeking clues to the writer's character.

His neighbor, Edna Lenington, had told him not to take too much stock in the pictures. Photographs are only as honest as the light and the photographer allow them to be. Still, Max had huddled for hours in the light of a kerosene lantern studying them.

No question that Catherine was pretty bone deep, not like some of the others. Max could tell the difference between a well-boned horse and a kid's pony all decked out with tassels and silver rigging. He would recognize her all right when she stepped off the stage.

Max ran a finger around his collar again. This thing would probably choke him before the stage arrived. Miss Catherine O'Dowd would pull into town looking for her husband and find him dead and flyblown on the boardwalk. Most likely, none of his friends would recognize him dressed as he was. They'd just let him lie there in the sun while the flies crawled across his eyes.

Max's mind skipped like a dust mote in the sun, settling for a moment on a glass of beer. Sure would hit the spot. Cold it would be from ice cut and stored last winter, and foamy, too. Max's mouth would have watered if there had been any juice left in him, but there wasn't, so he just stood there, a little more parched than before.

A yellowjacket buzzed up through the ovenlike air and settled on the drooping flowers. Max shook the bouquet, and the few remaining petals fell off and spun their way to his feet. Couldn't count on anything lasting in this country. Max offered the bouquet to his horse, but she turned up her nose and edged away.

Damn horse!

Probably was time for that beer. Even if the stage had edged over the horizon, there would still be plenty of time for a beer before it reached town, and there wasn't any sign of it, at all.

Max sighed, dropped the spent bouquet into the dust of the September street, and walked across to Millard's Saloon. It was cold inside compared to the heat outside, and dark. He paused a moment inside the front door, waiting for his eyes to adjust.

Wasn't much of a crowd. Few people could afford to spend an afternoon in the saloon. Doc Halvorson was there and Jimmy Pierce, a farmer from out on the Lone Pine. Swamper Smitty was sitting at *his* table, but he was there all the time, his absence more likely to be noticed than his presence.

Max sat down at the bar beside Jimmy, who nodded before returning his attention to the town's new weekly newspaper.

Jake Thomsen—bartender, bouncer, owner, and if he got in his cups, tenor—loomed in front of Max. Jake reminded Max of nothing so much as a bucket stuck on a whiskey keg. His head swelled into a neck that would never know a buttoned collar and continued down massive shoulders to a truly monumental stomach. A pair of bandy legs moved that mass around with amazing grace. Thomsen had bought Millard's from the original owner, Millard Smith, a haberdasher from Pennsylvania who came west with the homesteaders to make his fortune. Millard quickly saw that saloons were the only sure-fire business in Montana, and he built this one. But the less-than-robust Pennsylvanian had not reckoned with the rowdiness of the cowboys and homesteaders who frequented the place. It wasn't long before Millard was owner in name only. The bar opened when the first cowhand decided it should, and closed when the last drunk passed out. When the cowboys ran out of money, they demanded drinks on the house. Millard sold the establishment to Thomsen for a song and fled the prairie for another haberdashery in San Francisco.

Thomsen made it through his first day on the job without any trouble. His imposing size did wonders to quench the fighting spirits of the town rowdies. But that night, Big George Miller came in and ordered a beer on the house. Max had been sitting on the same stool and had seen the whole thing. Thomsen told Big George, nice and quiet like, that if he wanted a free drink, he should go to a wake, not a bar. George growled once and swung. He was a rib-breaking body puncher, and he hit Thomsen about five times with big roundhouse swings, but Thomsen didn't move. George eased up then until the punches were little more than slaps. Then he stopped and looked into Thomsen's eyes for the first time. Thomsen was grinning, and George knew he had made a big mistake. Max would never forget that moment. Big George started to cry, bawling like a baby. "Aw gawd, Jake, I'm sorry," he said. "I didn't mean nothing." Some of George's friends led him off, not a mark on anything but his pride.

From that night on, everyone knew Jake Thomsen was in charge at Millard's. Occasionally, somebody needed a refresher course, but never more than one.

The back bar was big, hand-carved mahogany, sporting a mirror. On more than one night Max had wished the mirror was elsewhere so he wouldn't have to watch his own foolishness. Now he could see nothing but Thomsen's white apron sprawled across his chest and belly like a Persian rug on a living room floor.

"Max," Thomsen said, extending a hand that seemed almost ladylike in comparison with the rest of him. "Congratulations."

"Thanks, Jake. She'll be in on the eleven fifteen."

Thomsen pulled an ornate hunting-cover watch from the expanse beneath his apron. "One thirty-seven. The eleven fifteen is right on time."

Both men chuckled.

"Beer?" Thomsen asked.

"Yeah."

Thomsen drew the beer from a keg beneath the bar, putting a one-inch head on it as he always did. "Nervous?"

"Why should I be nervous? When the stage comes in, I'm going to march down to the Patchuck house and marry a woman I've never met. Nervous? No, I'm not nervous."

Thomsen chuckled again.

"I'd be there if I could, you know."

"I know."

Max shifted his weight on the bar stool, easing the hitch he sometimes felt where he had broken his leg on the Big Dry. Then as though preparing himself for a religious mystery, Max tentatively took the handle of the beer mug. Cool it was, and smooth and wet. He raised the mug to his forehead and held it there until his head began to ache.

Max moved the mug to his lips. No! It wouldn't do to meet his wife with the smell of beer on his breath. No sense starting off on the wrong foot.

He slid the beer down to Pierce. The farmer looked up, nodded at Max, and then went back to the paper.

"How about a glass of water?"

"Sure," Max said with a grin.

"You want a shot of whiskey for a chaser?"

Max chuckled. "No, believe I'll take it straight." Then dropping a nickel on the bar, "Give Swamper a drink for me."

"I'll do that, but your money is no good here today. Bring the missus over after the wedding. I'll step out so she doesn't have to come in here, but I've got something for the two of you."

"I'll do that."

Max flipped the nickel several times, seeing how many times in a row he could make it come up heads. Then he fidgeted on the stool until Jake wandered back.

"Maybe you better go out and check on the stage."

"Yeah, maybe I better."

Max climbed down and stepped toward the door, a little more hastily than was his habit.

Outside, the sun hit him like a hammer. He took a short breath, holding it as he dived into the heat. As he walked across the street, a puff of dust rose into the still air each time his boots hit the ground.

The mare lifted her head to nicker as Max drew near but apparently thought better of it, and her head sagged again in the heat.

Max leaned against the hitching rack, assuming his watch over the southeastern horizon. Maybe the stage wouldn't come in today; maybe it broke a wheel or a horse went lame or the driver was too drunk to make the trip. Max would have had a hard time explaining why these thoughts gave him so much relief, but they did.

His eyes went to the horizon again. It would be tough to pick a moving stage out of the heat waves shimmering there.

And just as he was thinking that, the stage did appear, larger than life, writhing through the heat waves like a snake. There was no sound, no curses from the driver, no drumming of the horses' hooves, no creak of leather.

Maybe it was a mirage. The prairie wasn't above playing games with a man's mind.

But it was the stage all right. As it neared, he could hear Charlie Daniels cussing the horses, a steady stream of verbal abuse that would make any man or beast run for cover.

"Max?" Edna Lenington said. She was standing next to Max on the boardwalk staring up at him. He had been so lost in his thoughts that he hadn't heard her come up. "Max, you've got to be going now. You can't be here when she comes in."

He looked at Edna in amazement. Now that his fiancée was here, he couldn't even meet her?

"Max, she'll be dusty and dirty and tired from the trip. You go over to Millard's. I'll meet the girl and take her up to the Patchucks'. Zeb's there with the kids. I'll send him down. He wants to buy you a beer before the wedding, anyway."

She started to shoo Max off and then hesitated. "Just one beer. Don't you two get silly, now. Git! The stage is almost here."

Max scuttled across the street, feeling great relief that the meeting had been postponed and great anticipation of how that first beer would taste.

No sense waiting for Zeb. He could catch up when he got there.

CHAPTER 2

ANGER had been building in Catherine O'Dowd since the stage left Ingomar.

The driver, a foul-smelling lout whose gray beard was streaked brown at the corners by a constant dribble of tobacco juice, had managed to hit every bone-jolting bump and rut in the road. That was no mean accomplishment. There was more rut than road, and both were hidden in a blanket of dust thick as a feather comforter.

The driver drove as though he were pursued by the hounds of hell, laying the whip and an unending lexicon of foul language on the horses' rumps, the stage careening crazily across the track.

And behind the stage, a plume of dust spun into the air like smoke from a burning earth, inflamed by steel-rimmed wheels and horses' hooves. Dust filtered through the curtained windows of the stage, hanging almost motionless.

The stage company would hear about this. Miss Catherine O'Dowd would speak, and the company would listen. The wives of captains of industry like Maxwell Bass, were, by God, listened to. The ears of that filthy driver would burn as she told him who she was about to be, and what she thought of him. Ladies did not put up with such treatment, and Catherine O'Dowd was about to become a lady.

Lady! The sound of that was sweet as the scent of

heather on a soft breeze. Lady! There was precious little chance that she would have been called lady in her native Ireland, missus more likely. But by the end of the day, lady she would be.

Were it not for the fact that she was practicing the gentility necessary to that station, she would have called the driver to a stop and given him a tongue lashing that would sting more than that whip he was so fond of cracking.

Miss Catherine O'Dowd might be of little consequence to that foul creature in the driver's boot, but he would listen to Mrs. Maxwell Bass. Hat in hand, he would be, eyes averted as she sharply reminded him to take care when dealing with his betters.

Catherine knew about dealing with her betters. Once an heir to the estate on which her parents labored stopped outside the whitewashed stone cottage the O'Dowds called home. The boy and she were of like age, but he sat atop a blooded mare, dressed in the finest clothes Catherine had ever seen. And she stood barefoot in the mud, trying to hide the torn spots of her ragtag dress with her hands.

The young boy looked at her as though she were a creature beyond his ken, and she steeled herself to look him straight in the eye until he looked away. It was that day that she decided to leave Ireland.

Catherine was a patient girl. Whether she was born with that quality, or learned it over the next seven years is a matter of conjecture, and of little consequence. But patient she was, saving over those years a pitifully small purse, which she hid behind a stone in the fireplace. Sometimes, on those rare occasions when she was alone in the house, she would take the coins from their hiding place, hold them to her breast, and pray that she might leave Ireland before she was taken to wife.

And gradually, even though her feet still played across the cool, black soil of her native country, she began withdrawing from that place, preferring to live as a lady in her fantasies.

It was not that Catherine avoided her tasks. One cannot ignore obligations to family, no matter how helpless and unhappy one is. But when she was peeling potatoes for the evening meal, her mind would carry her beyond the hut to a place of blooded horses, fine clothes, and ladies and gentlemen.

Her mother would watch Catherine those times and wonder at the decorum with which her daughter held her chin, wonder if somehow she had been delivered of the wrong baby. Never had there been majesty in her own life, only drudgery and child-bearing. She began to dream then, too. Not much, only a small dream that her daughter would have a better life than she had had. But there was little time for fantasy in her life, and within moments she would turn her calloused hands to another of the unending tasks that defined her life.

Catherine's aspirations defined her as "different." The "differentness" was a shield, keeping the boys of the village at arm's length, their mothers cautioning them about girls who tended to daydream when their attention should be focused on more practical matters.

And perhaps it was her "differentness" that made Father O'Malley think of the O'Dowd girl, Catherine, after reading the letter from a wealthy Irish-American family who wanted a girl with the lilt of Old Eire in her voice to serve dinners at their mansion in Boston. The family would pay the girl's passage to America, the letter said, in return for three years' service.

Would she? Father O'Malley asked.

Would it not be sinful to turn down that which she had prayed for? Catherine answered.

Father O'Malley smiled and the bond was made.

Three years Catherine had spent in Boston, slowly coming to the realization that being a servant in America was not much different, after all, from being a tenant in Ireland. As those years crawled to a close, Catherine was filled with despondency.

But then came the advertisement!

Montana rancher and coal mine owner seeking younger woman with matrimony object of intentions. Interested parties may write Max Bass, General Delivery, Prairie Rose, Montana.

Prairie Rose, Montana! The name fairly sang of romance and adventure. She had written and rewritten her letter until it was in her finest hand, and in language fit for the wife of a Montana entrepreneur, language fit for a lady.

A lady!

The notion nudged Catherine out of her reverie, and her anger surged, filling her throat with bile. That driver would get his comeuppance when the stage company learned, as it would, how the wife of Max Bass had been jolted about.

"First time West?"

The question pulled Catherine's attention from the blistering speech she would make to the stage driver to the man sitting across from her.

She had noticed him when he boarded the stage in Ingomar. He was of medium height, a bit pudgy with the soft, white skin that better fits a woman than a man. In compensation, he had cultivated a wispy beard to put some hard edges and a little maturity to his visage. The attempt was a failure, like growing mold on an egg to make it more attractive.

"First time?" he continued.

"Why, yes, it is," she answered, the lilt of Ireland strong in her voice.

"Where you bound for?"

"My destination," Catherine retorted, with the appropriate sharpness reserved for louts who meddle in a lady's affairs.

"Sorry, no offense meant."

Catherine nodded.

"Me, I'm headed for Prairie Rose. Now there's a town for you. Isn't much yet, of course, but you just watch our smoke. Speakin' of which, do you mind?"

He pulled a cigar from a case in his coat and held it toward Catherine, awaiting her approval.

She nodded again, thinking the smell of a good cigar might be preferable to the dirty, dusty, baking air in the coach. He touched a match to the end of the stogie and sent a puff of smoke into the coach.

"Name's Phillips, Aloysius Phillips. Banker," he said, punctuating the statement with another puff of smoke, "part owner and president of the Prairie Rose Bank."

"President," he continued, with his self-satisfaction obvious in his tone, "of the Prairie Rose Commercial Club, too," he added, nodding for emphasis.

"It was me named Prairie Rose. Just like a flower unfolding on the prairie, I says. Prairie Rose it's got to be, I says, and they all saw how right I was. Smart men, they are in Prairie Rose."

Catherine decided to trip the strutting popping jay.

"Since, sir," she said, peering at him as though he were something she had found smeared on her shoe, "you are a businessman, perhaps you know of my fiancé, Maxwell Bass."

"By jingo, I knew it was you," Phillips retorted, slapping his knee. "Gents, I'd like you to meet Max Bass's mail-order bride. Came here all the way from Ireland, by way of Boston. Pretty little thing, isn't she though? Looks like Max snagged himself a keeper."

Catherine froze. She pretended that Phillips was not in the coach, that he had not spoken to her. But pallor spread across her face like snow sifting across a Montana pasture. That was burned away by a pink stain hot as a brand. Catherine O'Dowd, the daughter of an Irish peasant family, had been caught pretending to be something she wasn't, pretending that a letter from a man in Montana had enough magic in it to make a maid into a lady.

She had been discovered for what she was. A woman with so few prospects that she chased a promise all the way from Boston to Prairie Rose, Montana. No lady that. Just Catherine O'Dowd: peasant, maid.

Phillips was grinning. He knew he had smeared her soul with dirt. He reveled in that. Speak uppity to him, would she, this shanty-Irish, mail-order bride?

"Must not have been enough men in Boston," Phillips continued. "Or maybe there were too many?"

The banker blew a puff of smoke at Catherine, and for a moment, it obscured the sneer on his face, but only for a moment.

"Get my point?" he asked staring her full in the eyes.

And Catherine turned her face blindly to the window so the other passengers would not see the tear that coursed through the layer of dust on her face, leaving a streak of mud.

The driver banged on the roof of the coach with the

butt of his whip. "Prairie Rose, five minutes," he said, his voice disappearing behind the veil of dust the whip had dislodged from the ceiling.

Prairie Rose, Catherine thought, a blossom opening on the prairie. She tried very hard to conceal her tears from the other passengers, and they tried very hard to pretend they hadn't heard Phillips baiting her, hadn't seen her cry.

The remainder of the trip was in silence except for the creaking of leather, squeaking of wheels, drumming of hooves and the occasional pop of the driver's whip. The heat of Catherine's anger dried her tears, and she sat stony faced, waiting for the end of her journey.

"Whoa, you sonsabitches!" shouted the driver.

The stage lurched to a stop in a cloud of invective, the same way it had run. Even as he climbed off the seat, the driver continued his monologue. "Can't make these sway-backed, pea-brained, gas-passing horses move, and once you get 'em moving, you can't get 'em to stop. Spend half their time fightin' each other and the other half fightin' me."

Then louder, to the horse tender who had come with a fresh team, "Take good care of 'em, Billy. It was a good run."

An uneasy patter of laughter ran through the coach at the driver's words. The passengers rose stiffly and patted dust from their clothes. Last to leave the coach were Catherine and Phillips.

"Mr. Phillips," Catherine said. "I don't want you to leave with the wrong impression."

Phillips smirked. The tone in Catherine's voice was diffident, much more to the banker's liking. He settled in his seat, awaiting the apology due him.

"I just want you to know that nothing I said to you

was meant to convey my true feelings about what a pompous ass you are. Get my point?"

Then Catherine rammed her hat pin into the banker's leg. Phillips gasped, and Catherine leaned over until her nose was two inches from his. Her eyes, green as the sea on a sunny day, were lit with sparks.

"You move and I'll stick this pin into the bone. The doctor will have to remove it then, and I'll tell the town I was trying to protect myself from your advances. I don't think that would do your reputation much good, do you?"

Phillips shook his head, drops of sweat falling from the tip of his nose, little puffs of dust marking their arrival on his protruding vest.

"You should be kinder to ladies, Mr. Phillips. Don't you agree?"

Phillips nodded, eyes rolling back in his head as though he were about to faint.

"Speak to me again as you did today, Mr. Phillips, and I'll give the barbershop quartet in town a man who can sing high C."

By now sweat was running off the banker's face in rivulets, and his collar was smeared with mud.

"You may go now, Mr. Phillips," Catherine said, withdrawing the pin. He fled the coach, bent over, hand on his leg where Catherine had made her point.

Catherine stepped to the door, blinded for a moment by the harsh light of midday. As her eyes grew accustomed to the light, she realized that no man resembling the photograph she carried was waiting. Catherine had studied the photograph many times, seeking clues to the man who hid beneath. It was an open, honest face, the kind that people instinctively trust. There was determination, too, going to stubbornness along the line of the jaw, and a stiffness in the way he sat. Catherine could only guess whether that was because of an innate formality or simply because he wasn't accustomed to having his picture taken.

But how could the open, honest man in the picture leave his fiancée at the stage?

Catherine took two deep breaths, fighting desperately to control the panic she felt rising in her. Had it all been some cruel hoax? Had she been lured out to the prairies of eastern Montana by some false promise?

"Catherine? Catherine O'Dowd?"

Catherine's attention was pulled to a woman waiting on the boardwalk in front of the stage office. She was much older than Catherine, though perhaps not in years. Her face was brown and rough from too much sun, and her hands calloused and scarred from too much work. Still, she fairly glowed with excitement, and Catherine instinctively liked her.

"Name's Edna Lenington. Neighbor to Max . . . uh, Maxwell, I mean, Mr. Bass. He asked me to meet you so you could tidy up a bit before you two get together. That is before you two get married. I mean . . ." Chagrin spread over Edna's face. "Sorry, it's just that there isn't much that happens around here, and when it does, it's mostly bad. Something nice is . . . well, just so nice."

Catherine smiled. "You can't be any more excited than I am," she said.

Edna sent Catherine's bags ahead with two children and then motioned for Catherine to follow. "Few things you'll have to get used to out here," she said, stepping up the walk briskly. "The first is that there aren't many priests. Come around three or four times a year for weddings and baptisms and such. No one in town to take confessions, so you have to try a little harder to play it straight. Not that I think you wouldn't anyway. I mean . . . I didn't mean anything by that."

She stopped to take a breath and then opened up again. "Why, listen to me rattle on. I don't know what's got into me. I've been talking a blue streak since I met you, and I haven't let you get in a word. How was the trip?"

"It was just fine."

Those four words apparently salved Edna's conscience, and she continued, "I imagined that it would be. Zeb, me, and a half dozen kids came out in an immigrant car. Now, that's not near so fancy as traveling coach the way you did. I saw your tickets, you know. Max showed them to me. First class all the way, I says. Nothing but first class for my bride, he says.

"Oh, now I remember what it was that I was going to tell you. Father Tim has to leave this afternoon. Funeral up on Dead Sioux Creek. He has to go soon, so you and Max won't really have any break-in time to get to know each other. You'll have to be married today. In about thirty-five minutes."

Catherine stopped short on the boardwalk, but Edna continued several steps, talking to herself before she noticed she was alone.

"My word," she said. "Where did she go? Oh, there you are. . . ."

"We are to be wed this afternoon?"

"You are if you want a priest to do it."

"I do," Catherine said, resuming her walk. "I want everything to be nice and legal."

CHAPTER 3

THE first beer went down in a gulp, the second, too. Max had lingered a bit over the third, or was it the fourth, he couldn't remember. Now he was toying with his fifth or maybe sixth? No, it couldn't have been that many. Zeb couldn't stand more than about four mugs of beer without getting tipsy.

Max looked at his drinking companion. Zeb was sitting motionless on his stool, staring woodenly at the mirror behind the bar. Must have been more than four.

Then Max felt someone tugging at his sleeve. It was the Lenington's oldest boy, Hanford, or maybe next in line, Robert. All the Lenington children looked so much alike and were so close in age, it was difficult for Max to tell them apart.

"You better come now, Mr. Bass," Hanford or Robert said. "Miss O'Dowd is ready to see you. You have about fifteen minutes, Mama said, and then Miss O'Dowd has to get dressed for the wedding.

Max went cold-stone sober with panic. He couldn't go through with this. He had lured this woman, this stranger, to Prairie Rose with lies, representing himself to be something he wasn't. What chance did this marriage have? He was set in his ways and didn't know anything about women. There could only be trouble. Better that he just slip out the door and disappear.

But in the end he didn't. He took a deep breath and steeled himself for the task ahead just as he had always done. Come blizzards or heat or drought or prairie fires or fiancées, Max had always done what needed doing. And now that he was his own man, plotting the course of his life, he would not shrink from his duty. If a man did only the pleasant tasks God granted him, precious little would ever be done.

Max put his beer mug on the bar, and with the air of a man saying good-bye to what had been to make way for what would be, he slid off the stool to his feet.

Robert or Hanford was still trying to talk his father into leaving his perch, but he was having no luck.

Max reached out to pull Zeb off the stool.

"No, wait!" the Lenington boy said, taking Max's arm. "Dad," he said shaking the elder Lenington by the shoulders. "Ma is in the barn after your bottle. Little Zeb told her where it is, and she's after it."

Zeb's transformation to consciousness was not nearly so marked as Max's, but the boy's ploy got him on his feet, nevertheless.

"Edna, you stay away from that barn!" he yelled at the top of his voice. Zeb slowly realized where he was and what he had done. He was too drunk to be embarrassed, so he turned to the seated patrons and bowed as though he were a Shakespearean actor taking a curtain call. Then he staggered toward the door, flanked by his son and Max.

The sunshine outside seemed to drive a spike through Max's eyes and into his brain—the ache so severe his vision fluttered with it. Then the heat hit him and he stumbled, almost falling to the boardwalk.

Zeb was standing bolt upright, clinging to one of the hitching posts, his face bearing a look of complete bewilderment. Then he dropped to his knees and vomited over the edge of the walk, his belly emptying itself in gushes like water spewing from a rain pipe. As he struggled to his feet, a blush of pink spread across the pallor of his face.

Max thought Zeb might live if they could get him out of the heat, get him up to the Patchucks' where the priest and the rest of the Leningtons and this stranger from Boston were waiting.

It was the longest walk Max had ever made, longer even than that time on the Big Dry when that spooky son of a bitching bay pitched him off a rim edge into a nest of boulders below. Bone sticking through his leg it was. Through his pants, too. But he dragged himself the twelve miles back to the ranch. He had no choice. It was either that or die alone on the prairie. Nothing scared Max so much as the thought of lying wide-eyed in dead disbelief until some magpie came and picked holes in his skull where his eyes had been. So Max had crawled the twelve miles, sucking every breath and holding it like a talisman, dragging one dead leg behind him. He would walk to the Patchucks' half-drunk through this god-awful heat for the same reason: *He didn't want to die alone on the prairie.*

The sidewalk, the buildings, the horizon spun together into a viscous collage that Max waded through as though he were chest deep in a vat of honey. After what seemed to be hours, the trio was standing in front of the Patchucks', Max reaching toward the door to knock, to set his destiny in motion. But just before his knuckles touched wood, the door opened and Edna peered out, consternation plain on her face.

"Come in! Come in! She won't be ready for a few minutes, and that will give me time to pump some coffee into you."

Max lurched inside, and Edna guided him to a chair,

leaving her son to find a chair for his father. Inside the home out of the heat, Max's mind began to clear again, adrenaline chasing alcohol from his body.

"Edna, I would dearly love a cup of coffee."

"Not yet. I'll get you some water and you rinse your face. Run a comb through your hair and straighten that collar, too. You are about to meet your wife, Max. Best get yourself straightened out."

"You're right, Edna," Max said so softly she heard only a murmur. "I'd best get myself straightened out."

"It's time, Max. She's in the parlor."

Edna's voice sent a chill down Max's spine. As the adrenaline surged through his body, he was acutely aware of the sounds, smells, and tension that circulated through the Patchuck home.

He rose, his legs shaky at first, shakier still as he marched into the parlor to the beat of his heart booming in his chest. As he stepped through the entryway, his eye was drawn in the dim light to a lamp on one end of the couch. And there, in that golden globe of light, was Catherine O'Dowd. Catherine was perhaps the most beautiful creature Max had ever seen. She rose from the couch with a grace that Max thought God had reserved for creatures of the wild: the deer, the antelope, the fox, and the wolf. Her smile, set as it was in a face underlined by a gentle, yet strong chin, held promise. Green eyes so deep a man could step into them were set wide in the face, framed by high cheekbones.

It was difficult to fathom Catherine's figure beneath the dress of the day. A more discerning eye than Max's might have noticed that she was a bit sturdy, more the wild rose that paints Montana creek banks pink in the spring than a pampered houseplant.

But to Max, struck dumb in the parlor, Catherine O'Dowd was without fault.

Catherine had raced through her toilet at the Patchuck house, the preparation stilling the anxiety she felt. When all was done, she had arranged herself in the darkened parlor to her best advantage, the yellow light of the kerosene lamp softening the lines of exhaustion on her face. She meant to remain seated when Max entered the room, to greet him as the ladies of the house in Boston greeted their guests, but that affectation was lost in her need to see this man she was about to marry.

Maxwell Bass was of more than average height, perhaps a little under six feet. His face, baked by summer suns and scoured by winter winds unfolded like a topographical map of Montana. The rugged ridges of his eyebrows, nose, and chin dominated the face as the Beartooths, Missions, Crazies, and Spanish Peaks dominate Montana. The spaces between were wrinkled here and there with laugh lines and folds marking the perplexed expression he adopted when considering whether cattle should be moved or the man across the poker table from him had one pair or two.

"How do you do, Mr. Bass?" she said. "I am Catherine O'Dowd."

Max had spent hours considering what he would say when he met his wife. Then he practiced those words, speaking into an empty prairie wind until he could recite the speech in his sleep, and he often did, the sound of his voice awakening him.

But now, when he needed those words worse than he had needed anything in his life, he could not pull them from his memory. He stood mute and desperate, thankful when "Howdy, ma'am" tumbled from his mouth.

Max couldn't remember the last time he had blushed, but he blushed now, the heat spreading across his face. Knowing that his face was red made him blush even more.

Finally Max spoke, and when he did, it all came out in a rush. "Ma'am, I don't know what you expected, but I don't likely measure up. To speak in my defense, you should know that I'm a hard worker, none harder. Anyone around here can tell you that. And I'm out here because I want to be, not because there's no place else for me to go. That's the edge I've got."

Max paused, his eyes searching her face.

"Ma'am, it ain't going to be easy. I want you to know that. And if you don't like what you see, you don't have to go through with this. I'll buy you a ticket back to Boston right now if you want."

It was Catherine's turn now to probe Max's face. Then she spoke. "I believe I'll stay."

Max's grin left the kerosene lamp pale by comparison.

"But one thing, Mr. Bass," she said firmly. "Don't say 'ain't.' "

Max nodded.

The marriage ceremony went by in a blur; Max remembered the words in bits and pieces. "Dearly beloved . . . the union of husband and wife in heart, body, and mind is intended by God for their mutual joy . . . for the help and comfort given one another in prosperity and adversity . . . therefore marriage is not to be entered into unadvisedly or lightly, but reverently, deliberately, and in accordance with the purposes for which it was instituted by God . . . for richer and poorer . . . to love and to cherish. This is my solemn vow."

And afterward the reception and the accordion and the drinks and knowing winks from the other men and the swirl of women's dresses flashing like patches of prairie flowers in a spring wind . . .

And still more we-wish-you-wells; come-see-us; if-there-is-anything-we-can-do.

Max felt trapped. He wasn't good in crowds—never had been. Anything more than a bunkhouse full made him edgy. A party like this darn near rendered him unconscious.

But finally, when Max thought he had had enough socializing to last him a lifetime, the crowd began to drift toward the door—wives aware, even if their husbands weren't, that the affair had to be curbed before the whiskey robbed the men's reason.

Max spotted Miss O'Dowd—no, Mrs. Bass—across the room in a knot of chattering women. He edged over to the group, feeling awkward as always around decent women.

"Ma'am," he said, touching the sleeve of her dress and then, realizing what he had done, jerking his hand back as though he had touched a hot stove.

"Ma'am, I think it's time for us to go."

Catherine nodded, trying to ignore the twittering that tripped through the group.

She was as apprehensive as Max but for different reasons. She had stepped into the Patchuck home as a celebrity of sorts. Every eye was upon her as she stood before the priest. Then she had been the star of a party held in her honor.

But now she would be stepping through the door, and once she reached the other side she would be Mrs. Bass. Missus. And the course of her life from that point forward would be set by everything implicit in that.

Max was waiting for her on the porch, the apology tumbling from him as though his soul depended on it. "I hope you don't mind. I was going to hire a carriage, but I get into town so seldom, and I needed some things, and . . . and I didn't know if you would be going home with me."

"Don't you have a carriage, Mr. Bass?"

"Nope, didn't have any need of one . . . before now."

"No matter," she said. "But perhaps I should change into something more appropriate for a buckboard. You could pick up the things you need and meet me back here."

Max nodded, and the two fled from each other with a great sense of relief.

CHAPTER 4

MAX went over the list in his mind. First to the general store for one-by-fours and white-lead paint. Then to the Baldry place to pick up fifty-or-so hens and a few roosters.

The Baldrys had been surprised when Max ordered the birds. It was too early to butcher, and too close to winter to expect eggs much longer. Max didn't tell them why he needed the chickens. That was between him and Catherine, and he hadn't even told her yet.

When Max returned to the Patchucks', Catherine was sitting in a rocker on the porch. Her luggage—pitifully little for the accumulation of a lifetime—sprawled beside her.

Max pulled the mare to a stop and tipped his hat.

"I've got it all," he said.

Catherine nodded, not realizing all he meant by that statement.

Max stepped down and offered Catherine his hand as she climbed into the wagon seat. Then he loaded her baggage next to the makeshift chicken pen, climbed aboard, and wheeled the wagon around, walking the mare down the street to Millard's.

"Back in a second," Max said as he got down and disappeared into the bar.

The crowd at Millard's was considerably larger than it had been that afternoon. Swamper was still there, of course, and Thomsen. Jimmy Pierce's newspaper lay on the bar, but he had drifted off to one place or another. Most of the newcomers were men from the wedding. Primed punch had pointed them to Millard's more certainly than any compass.

As Max stepped through the door, Harry Jensen lifted his glass and bellowed, "I'm buying one for Max," and that was followed by a chorus of "me, too's."

Max shook his head. "Miss Catherine's waiting in the wagon."

"She might as well learn to wait," Jensen shouted. "She'll do plenty of it." It was whiskey talk, and a ripple of whiskey laughter spread through the saloon.

Max shrugged and stepped up to the bar, and the men cheered. They were far enough into their cups to appreciate declarations of independence, particularly if they themselves didn't have to fight the civil war.

The men surged toward the bar, and Max's teeth bared as he noticed the banker Phillips standing in a little knot of men.

Max held the banker in contempt, and Phillips reciprocated with a vehemence that made his teeth hurt. The bad blood was bone deep and as old as their acquaintance, but the feud had been exacerbated by an incident that occurred not long after Phillips became president of the Prairie Rose Bank.

And every time Phillips saw Max, that time came back to him clear as the glasses hanging on the back bar. Phillips had just arrived in town, and he had spent a few weeks studying the populace. Hayseeds, he thought, and not two dollars to rub together among the lot of them. But they had land—mile after mile after mile of land.

The key to his fortune, the banker decided, was to separate these rubes from their land.

Phillips had spent the next couple of weeks poring

over county records, determining which homesteads were worth stealing. That done, he set his nefarious mind to plotting.

The idea had come to him one night while he was soaking in the bathtub at the Harris boarding house. The flyer he was reading cautioned bankers to beware of those who wanted to poke pipes into the pockets of oil that underlay the Montana prairie. Some of these oil men, the flyer said, were as slippery as the gushers they were looking for.

Phillips's forehead furrowed as he studied the flyer, and then the corners of his mouth twitched into a smile. A moment later, Mrs. Harris was surprised at a peal of laughter from the banker's room. (Phillips was not a particularly jocular man.)

The plan was brilliant in its simplicity. First a letter to cousin Milburn. Milburn would collect some "oil men" who would spend a few weeks poking around the land bordering Pishkin Creek. They would peek through surveyor transits, set pins, and occasionally dig a hole. Asked what they were doing, they would answer cryptically that they were seeking signs.

Once all the ranchers in the area were properly primed, the oil crew would leave for a couple of weeks to allow the rumors to build and swirl along the banks of Pishkin Creek, and then the advertisements would begin appearing in the *Prairie Rose Printer:*

Eastern oil interests have discovered major oil field in Prairie Rose area. First for the state. Huge development seen. People will flock to area by thousands. Prairie Rose will prosper and become major Montana city. Those interested in lining their pockets with oil money may attend meeting seven o'clock in the evening of August 19 at Millard's emporium. Free beer for the men. Free sarsaparilla for the children. Free coffee for all, and free money for the taking. New day on Prairie Rose horizon.

Milburn had collected as august a body of con men as ever breathed Montana's big sky, and the banker wanted to cry Bravo as he watched them play the crowd.

"As all of you good people are aware," the pitch began, "oil is the product of vegetation and animals living long ago on these plains."

The crowd nodded collectively. They were not about to admit their ignorance of how oil was formed to these big-city oil men.

"And as all of you know, fossils indicate where these oil-producing plants and animals lived."

Nods again.

"And here we have some fine examples of fossils we have discovered along Pishkin Creek," one oil man said, dumping a sackful of ancient shells and bones on the table.

Some of the people in the audience whispered smugly to their neighbors: "Yup. I figured them fossils were a good sign. Said so all along."

Excitement was building, and when the people began to fidget in their seats, the oil men slipped in the sting. If the good people of Pishkin Creek were to invest five hundred dollars apiece, the operaton could be under way within a week, and Prairie Rose would be on its way to riches.

The air exited 150 sets of lungs in one collective sigh. It was just like everything else. You had to have money to make money. Opportunity was walking right out the front door, and no one there had legs long enough to trip it.

Phillips let desperation build for a moment, and then

stood: "Good people of Prairie Rose. These men have excited me with the prospect of new wealth for all of you and for this community, which I hold so dear.

"I will not let this great opportunity slip through your fingers just because some of you may be suffering temporary financial problems. So I will march with you over to the bank right now—no banker's hours for the president of the Prairie Rose Bank—and give you money to invest in this worthwhile enterprise.

"You can pay me back when the oil payments begin rolling in a few months from now. Don't think of this as a loan. Think of it as an advance on the fortunes you will be depositing in my bank in the coming good years."

Then Milburn stood. "I will, by God, take some of that free money."

"Me, too's" were popping up around the crowd like corn in a hot pan, and Phillips smiled to himself.

All his life, he'd been looking for the perfect con, and now he'd found it. He would lend the ranchers a quarter of their land's worth on a short-term loan. Half that money would go to cousin Milburn and the phony oil men and half to himself. It was, after all, his idea.

The oil men would skip town. The banker would be mortified, but what could he do? He had lent the bank's money, and he had to collect it. So he would foreclose ranches for a quarter of their value. Then he would use money from the swindle to buy the ranches from the bank—through Milburn, of course—and sell them in a year for four times his investment, which he had stolen from the ranchers in the first place. The bank's board of directors would praise him for protecting their interests by ensuring the loans were well backed with collateral, and in three years the banker would be lying on the beaches of the south of France, drinking wine and looking for the women on those pictures he kept in his room.

But then that damn Maxwell Bass stood, and every eye in the place focused on him. "If this is such a good investment, why doesn't the bank just lend the money to the oil men?"

Damn! Who would have thought that one of these hayseeds would come up with that, but when Phillips rose, he was all smiles. "The Prairie Rose Bank is committed to the good people of this community. We want to *share* the wealth."

And Max grinned. "In my experience," he said, "a banker is about as anxious to share the wealth as a coyote is to share chickens."

Laughter roared through the room, releasing the excitement and tension of the past few minutes, and in that respite, the people began to rethink the proposition.

"Suppose," Zeb Lenington asked, "you want a mortgage on our places? What if there isn't any oil?"

That and other questions killed the scam as quickly as it had kindled, and with it, Phillips's dreams of the ladies of France. That son of a bitching cowpoke had as much as stolen the banker's money, and Phillips had vowed to get even. He was still biding his time.

Phillips was thinking about that now as he limped to the bar. He was thinking, too, about the hole Max's bride had poked in his leg that afternoon.

The banker was a careful man. His opinions were usually delivered secondhand, but his natural caution had washed away two whiskies ago, and he was ready to tell that son of a bitch Bass what he thought of him and that high and mighty "lady" from Boston.

Phillips pulled himself to his full height and sneered,

"I'd like to know what kind of woman would come clear out here to marry a man like you."

There was silence broken only by the whisper of necks against stiff collars as the men turned to watch. And now that the banker realized the magnitude of what he had done, there was no one more intent on that question than he.

Max eased his beer to the bar as though it were thin shelled and fragile. Then he stepped off the stool and walked stiff-legged to Phillips.

The banker's eyes were wide and wild.

Max's face was hard as Beartooth granite.

"No man talks about my wife like that." Then his hands moved so fast the banker saw only a blur, and he waited helplessly for the blow.

Max's hands came together, *crack!*, a half inch from the banker's nose. He had only clapped his hands, but Phillips recoiled as though he had been struck. He stumbled back, and a chair caught him at the back of the knees. He tripped and crashed into a table, dumping glasses, cigar butts, and himself on the floor.

Max was still on his way back to the bar when the laughter struck like a thunderclap in a summer rainstorm. The banker scrambled to his feet and scuttled red-faced to the door, pelted on all sides by the derision of the men in the saloon.

He slunk out the door and hurried toward his office. Every step of the way, he vowed he would make Max Bass rue the day he had humiliated Aloysius Phillips.

Max choked down the beer, motioned to Thomsen, and a moment later the two of them appeared at the front door of the saloon, Max tugging Thomsen toward the wagon as awkwardly as a rowboat trying to tow a river steamer.

Thomsen was squinting against the light, but the moment Catherine fleshed out her silhouette, he smiled his approval.

"Jake, this is her. This is . . . my wife, Catherine O'Dowd . . . I mean, Catherine Bass."

"Ma'am," Thomsen said. "I'm thinking Max got the better of the deal.

Max grinned like a man showing off a prize heifer at the remark, but Catherine stiffened.

"There was no transaction, Mister Jake," she said, drawing out the mister until it stung.

"Jake Thomsen's the name, ma'am," he said, cocking his head the way he sometimes did when deep in thought. "Didn't mean to offend.

"Got a little something here for you and Max." With that he hoisted a hogshead into the back of the wagon, lifting a corner of the red cloth cover to reveal a bottle of champagne in a bed of ice. "Hope you enjoy it."

Thomsen waved off their thanks and said, "Suppose you're anxious to get to your new home."

"Oh, yes," Catherine said, brightening. "In his letters, Mr. Bass told me about the coal mine and the cattle and how the sun rises on one edge of the ranch and sets on the other."

Max cut in, "I didn't have time to tell her everything, but we'll be there quick enough."

"Quicker than you might think," Thomsen said, turning a quizzical eye on Max. Then he said to Catherine, "Remember who I am, ma'am. If I can ever do anything, let me know. I call Max friend."

"Thank you, Mr. Thomsen, I shall keep that in mind."

"And ma'am, that champagne bottle isn't very fancy, but it's good wine, the best I could buy—in Montana, anyhow. Sometimes the best wine comes in plain bottles."

"And sometimes a man blows across the mouth of a jug and thinks he's making music," Max retorted with a grin.

"You've got me there," Thomsen said.

Despite the smile, Max felt uneasy. Wouldn't be long before he pulled the buckboard to a stop on his ranch and Catherine would know. He wasn't looking forward to that—not even a little bit.

It isn't good to travel midday on the Montana prairie in summer. There is the heat, of course, always the heat except on those rare occasions when thunderheads boil over the horizon and drench the land with rain or run hail like a rasp over it.

Nobody travels then. Fine dust that billows in the heat turns to glue when wet, and wheels grow thick and fat and high. Horses pick up buckets of gumbo and walk as though on mud stilts. Mud quells the spirit that sprouts in the rare prairie rains.

Midday, the sun shines straight down and washes the prairie out. Color, contour, and distance are lost to glare and heat waves. These are the beauty of the plains, and midday hides them from the eye.

Max drove the wagon in desperation. He wanted to speak to his wife, tell her the truth about his ranch and his mine. He wanted to tell her not to judge the prairie until she had learned its secrets, glimpsed the beauty it hid from strangers; not to judge him until she knew what he would be, not what he was.

But he couldn't do that.

He had used lies to lure her to Prairie Rose as a

hunter uses a whistle to pull an elk to his rifle. Normally, he was not a man who lied, but he had lied greatly in this, and he had lied to a woman who deserved more than he would ever be.

He wondered how those green-flecked eyes would look at him when she saw the ranch, when Catherine O'Dowd learned that she had married a liar.

And on they rode in sun-drenched silence; a wagon laden with lumber and whitewash and chickens and guilt, trailing a plume of white dust across the Montana prairie.

About fifteen miles out of town at Myer's Corner, Max clucked the mare off the main track to ruts leading to his home.

Catherine asked, "Here?" and Max nodded. During the ride, only that word had been spoken between them, each hating the silence; each afraid to break it. They crossed a rocky creek ford and climbed the other side, water cascading from the wagon's wheels. Max pulled the rig to a stop.

"Is that your creek, Mr. Bass?"

"Some of it."

"What's it called?"

"Pishkin."

Catherine's brow wrinkled, and Max explained.

"Blackfeet. Means *buffalo jump.* Used to be that Indians would start a herd of buffalo running and drive 'em right off a bluff upstream from here. Spill off the edge like a river running brown in the spring.

"If they tried to stop, the weight of the animals behind would push them over. Once they started running, it was certain they'd wind up on the edge of that bluff."

Max wiped his forehead with his sleeve.

"Sometimes, it seems that way with people, too. Start

running one way and you can't turn back, not even if you know what's waiting up ahead."

Catherine's eyes searched the horizon, looking for the bluff.

The country was not much different from what they had traveled through that afternoon. A range of hills topped by a slab of sandstone and painted dark here and there with trees and shadows lay like a wall to the north. The creek nourished a meandering stream of green, struggling against the heat. Off to the west, the land had been broken and planted in wheat, stubble shining gold against the sun. And just over the lip of the hill that marked the course of the creek stood a massive cottonwood. It stood alone on the prairie, and Catherine couldn't help but wonder what had caused it to grow here, so distant from any of its kind. The branches, some of them thick as a fat man's waist, spread in regal welcome.

But then Catherine's attention was turned from the tree to an inverted, galvanized tub sitting on the prairie. And poking through a hole in the tub's bottom was a stovepipe.

"Mr. Bass, what is that?"

But Max didn't answer. Instead, he unhitched the mare, more intent on his task than there was any reason to be.

"Taking the mare down to the creek to water. Want to come along?"

Catherine nodded and a moment later they were edging down the steep hill. Catherine's shoes were designed more for sidewalks than sidehills, and she reached for Max's arm. He walked stiffly, as though he were carrying something very valuable, or very dangerous.

When they reached the creek, Catherine gasped in delight. The giant cottonwood and the tall cut that marked the course of the creek shaded a park with grass as green as any that graced the fields of Ireland. A wall of sandstone marched along the opposite side, as though God were bent on shielding the beauty of the place from the harshness of the sun. And down through the middle of the bottom ran the creek, water kicking up its heels on a sandstone stage.

"Why, it's beautiful, Mr. Bass."

Max said nothing, thinking the bottom paled in comparison to the look on Catherine's face.

"Oh, look!"

Catherine was pointing to the cottonwood. About twenty feet up, a massive branch butted sideways forming a canopy over the creek bottom, and hanging from that branch by two long chains was a porch swing. Catherine ran to it like a little girl. She stood there a moment, admiring it, then sat down on the double chair and began pumping the swing into long slow arcs through the cool air and out over the creek.

Max stood on the bank, holding the mare's reins while she drank. His eyes were fixed on Catherine, and the flash of her hair as she swung through ragged patches of sunlight streaming through the shadow.

Catherine felt Max's eyes, and looked up. She was embarrassed then and stopped pumping until the swing settled to a stop. She stepped down, walking across the bottom to Max.

"Did you make that for me?"

Max nodded, and her smile was bright as the sunlight shining on her hair.

"I shall ride out here every day to sit in it beside this

brook." Another flash of smile and then, "Do we have time for me to explore this place?"

"We have time," Max said. He waited then, stiffly at attention as an accused man awaits the jury's verdict. Still he jerked a bit as her voice floated back to him.

"Oh, Mr. Bass, come see what I have found."

Max followed a faint trail through the bottom. Catherine was just past a bend in the creek. The walls were steep there, opening into a broad sun-drenched bottom of ten or so acres.

"Look," Catherine said as she heard Max approaching. "Someone has dug a hole."

And indeed, someone had, straight back into the hillside. Steps roughly formed from sandstone led steeply to the blanket-draped entrance ten feet or so above the bottom.

Catherine had already climbed the steps and was waiting by the blanket.

"Do you think it's all right to look inside?"

Max swept the blanket aside, and she stepped in. It was cool there and dark, but Max's hand brushed against the bail of a kerosene lantern, and he lit it, the pale light casting the dugout in heavy shadow. It was obvious that the dugout had been lived in. There was a bed of sorts—a straw-filled mattress on a frame of rough-hewn lodgepole pine—against one wall. An equally rough-hewn, blanket-draped table stood in the middle of the room.

The floor was wall-to-wall canvas; muslin hung from the ceiling to catch any falling dirt. There was nothing deceptive in the scene. It was an obvious attempt to make the best of a bad situation.

"Do you suppose someone is actually living here?" Catherine asked in a whisper.

"People have lived in worse."

"But not in America, not even in Ireland. This must be what you call a squatter. What will you do now? Will you tell him to move on?"

"No, I don't think so."

"I wonder what kind of man—he must be a man, no woman would stay here—would think about digging a hole to live in."

"Timber is scarce around here," Max explained. "In the summer the sun makes ovens of most houses, and winter winds blow right through a cabin. Some people build soddies. This is better than a soddy—warmer, anyway."

"But it's dark, even on a day like this, and closed in. There is nothing to see here but shadows, and the air is musty and dead. It's more like an animal's den than a home."

"Suits some."

"Look, a trunk!"

And then before Max could say anything, Catherine had lifted the lid. Inside were clothes: long johns, flannel shirts, and denim pants. There was a rawhide lariat, a .44 Colt, letters, and mounted in the inside of the trunk lid, a picture.

"Mr. Bass, please bring the lantern closer."

Max did, and with the light shining full on the photograph, Catherine could see that it was her own picture!

The realization struck her then, and she turned wide-eyed to Max.

"No!" she said, her voice filled with dread.

Max couldn't look her in the eye. He stood accused by that single word—no! And then in a voice drained of all emotion, all hope, Max whispered, "Yes."

The anger rose in Catherine and she spat out her fury. "Mr. Bass, if you had lived in Ireland, Saint Patrick would have kept the snakes and driven *you* out!" Then her anger broke like the North Sea against the Irish shore, and her head sank to her breast.

"Go now. Leave me alone in this snake pit you call home. Leave me to consider my foolish pride and ambition. Leave me alone."

Max walked toward the blanket door of his dugout, attempting to put some pride into his step although he could find none in his soul at that moment, but the effort was more than he could bear. He slunk toward the door.

It was bright outside, as though a curious world had focused a light on this devious two-legged creature to probe the depth of his perversion. Max's breath left him in one long sigh, and he had no more energy than a deflated balloon.

But there was work. Always there was work, and Max fled to it for refuge.

In town, the banker was still at work. The two tellers and the bookkeeper stayed nearly half an hour after the five o'clock closing time, waiting for Phillips to emerge from his office. Phillips usually left the bank at two, never later than three, and then set up shop at Millard's. He had never before been in the bank at closing time, and his employees didn't know now if they should leave or wait until he dismissed them.

But finally, they pulled the shades and slipped quietly out the door. Phillips had been in a miserable mood this afternoon, and it was safer for them to take a chance he would be feeling better tomorrow than risk intruding tonight.

The banker was singularly occupied. In his office, he pored over every account, every loan for mention of Maxwell Bass as borrower or even cosigner. But there was none.

That son of a bitch had never borrowed a penny from the bank and never deposited a nickel in it. As impossible as that seemed, the proof was in the books.

Phillips gritted his teeth. If Bass had owed money, the banker would have a stick to poke him where it hurts—in the pocketbook. But there was nothing.

The banker sat at his desk, grinding his teeth. Bass had a soft spot—everyone does. But where was it?

And then the corners of Phillips's mouth twitched into a perverse smile. Bass had accounts with the merchants in town. He had to. Paychecks come in twice a year for ranchers, not twice a month. And all the merchants owed the bank money. The banker would cut Bass off at the pockets and then wait with relish for that son of a bitch to come in, hat in hand.

Phillips was chuckling to himself as he stepped out of his office into the empty bank. His eyes narrowed for a moment when he realized his employees had sneaked off at the stroke of five o'clock, leaving their boss to labor alone. He'd teach them a thing or two about a full day's pay for a full day's work. He'd wait until the bank was full of customers tomorrow before he told those shirkers what he thought of them. Word would spread through town about how the bank president dressed down his malingering employees. That thought coaxed another smile to the banker's face, and the smile widened as Phillips realized that he had time for a beer before Mrs. Harris put on dinner at the boarding house.

It wasn't a bad day at all, when you could go home at night looking forward to the next morning.

CHAPTER 5

MAX took the mare downstream to the natural corral carved out of the sandstone slab lining each bank of the creek. He had run posts and poles across either end of the enclosure, leaving a fifteen-foot gate on the near end. It was there he had put up the tall grass that grew along the creek, cutting it and waiting until the sun dried it before he built the haystack. Stack hay too wet and it burns—spontaneous combustion. Stack it too dry and the leaves and seeds and food value leach out of it. Max's hay was just about right.

The mare nickered when she smelled the other horses downstream from the corral. After the wheat was harvested, Max had turned out his pair of Percherons to graze on the grass that grew along the creek and the windswept hill to the north. Most of Max's homestead of 640 acres, a square mile, was still in grass and would remain that way.

But the horses had become accustomed to the daily feedings of hay and oats, and they lingered around the corral, awaiting Max's ministrations.

Instead, he picked up a couple of rocks and chucked them at the animals, yelling and waving his arms until they reluctantly trotted away. There was precious little hay and rolled oats for the winter. Foolish to feed horses now when they could just as well feed themselves.

Max tried to bury himself in his work, but there was too little to do today, and his mind skipped back to the scene in the dugout. He was leaning against a pitchfork, thinking about that, when he heard her voice, hard against the sound of the creek.

"Mr. Bass!"

She was standing at the road beside the creek, dressed for travel with her trunk at her feet. Max wondered how she had managed to drag the heavy trunk that far by herself, and then he was filled with dread. He didn't want to look into those eyes again, hear the pain in her voice.

The day was cooling. It was that special time when the day surrenders to the night. Big, brassy, and bright under the sun, Montana turns magic at twilight, sighing contentedly before retiring.

But Max was not content as he walked to Catherine.

"I'm ready to go."

"Ma'am?"

"I'm ready to take you up on your offer. I would like a ride back to Prairie Rose and fare back to Boston."

"You didn't take that offer. We're married now, for better or worse."

"What?" Catherine snarled, the anger bubbling out of her. "You brought me here on a lie. If you think I will honor this . . . this marriage, you are even slower of wit than you appear. Do you really think I will live in a hole in the ground like a snake? Do you think that I am content to spend the rest of my life denning up with the likes of you? Perhaps you find the thought of that acceptable, but I do not. Neither do I, Mr. Bass, find you acceptable."

Max could feel the color rising in his face. Twice this day she had done that to him. When he replied, his voice was low and taut. "Madam," he said, his anger overriding his soft drawl, "before you get too high and mighty, you might remember a few things. I did lie in that newspaper ad, and I lied in those letters, too. That doesn't come easy to me. But you didn't marry a ranch or a coal mine or money. You married a man. After you saw me in town, I gave you a chance to go back to Boston, but you chose to stay here. I was acceptable to you then. You stood before a priest and swore that. You didn't tell the priest that you would marry me if I had a ranch and a coal mine. You said you would marry *me,* and by God, that's what you did. You made your bed, and now you're going to lie in it!"

Catherine gasped. "Mr. Bass," she hissed, "if you bed me tonight, so help me God, I will kill you. The first time you turn your back on me, the first time I catch you asleep, I will kill you!"

The unleashed vehemence drove Max back a step. Never had he seen unbridled anger like that without blood being shed.

"Now, you wait a minute," Max said. "I didn't say anything about bedding you, although you are my legal, lawful wife, and I have the right."

"No!" Catherine barked. "I have the right," and she swung it, *smack,* against Max's face.

The blow took Max by surprise, and he was surprised, too, at how much it stung. His anger rose like a winter storm.

"Madam," he said low and deep and ugly, "if you were a man, I'd . . . I'd. . . ."

"If *you* were a man," Catherine interrupted, "you wouldn't have to order your women through the mail."

"And if you were a lady," Max growled, "you wouldn't run halfway across the country at the first scent of money. There is a name for women who choose their men by the thickness of their wallet."

Catherine cocked her fist.

"If you hit me again, I will likely forget you are a woman."

This time Catherine backed off a step. They stood there glaring at each other, hearts hammering. And then the anger left Max, and he looked away, ashamed of himself: for losing his temper and threatening Catherine, for lying, for asking a woman to share his pitiful existence. When he looked at Catherine she was as pale as he felt. She wouldn't meet his eyes.

"I'm sorry," Max said, and he was. "I think we need to talk this thing over."

"We can talk it over on the way back to Prairie Rose."

"I can't take you back to Prairie Rose tonight. It's too far. You'll spend the night here." When Catherine bridled, he continued, "Now I didn't mean anything by that. I won't bother you.

"I have to take care of the chickens. If you would fix us dinner, it would be a big help. There's an icehouse just up that little side coulee above the dugout. There's some potatoes and some lard and some deer in there. . . ."

"Mr. Bass, I will fix you dinner. That much. Nothing more."

Max nodded and climbed toward the wagon on shaky legs. Marriage sure as hell wasn't all it was cut out to be.

There was nothing really that Max could do for the chickens. They were as safe as he could make them in the wagon bed, but he wanted to be alone, away from the lies he had told and the hatred in Catherine's eyes. He jury-rigged a roof over the wagon box, hoping it would keep coyotes and skunks off the chickens until morning when he could build a proper chicken house and pen.

Max climbed into the wagon and sat there waiting for the day to die. The afternoon sun was painting the sky with colors subtle as a young woman's blush. There is a serenity that settles over the land then, drawing animals from the cover that hides them during the day. Deer edge from coulees and browse onto sidehills clothed with sage and juniper. Coyotes, always on the run to fill their bellies with mice and rabbits and chickens, sing to themselves and their prey: Hear me, rabbit. Shake in your hiding place, for I am coming to fill my belly with your quivering flesh.

Max slid off the wagon seat. It was time to deal with Catherine now. He wouldn't tell her everything. She would likely run if he did, but he had best tell her something about his goals, his dreams, if he wanted her to stay in Prairie Rose. He took a deep breath and walked toward the dugout through the deepening darkness.

Catherine had found the icehouse. It had double doors, leading to an interior, rough, but in many ways built better than the dugout. Max had lined the walls with sandstone slabs hauled down from the rimrock. The roof was made of rough lumber, lined with tarpaper. The back of the icehouse was stacked roof high with blocks of ice that had been cut the preceding winter from the creek and covered with dark sawdust. There were sacks of potatoes stacked on the near wall, away from the ice; hanging from a hook in the middle of the ceiling was a hind quarter of venison.

Catherine didn't realize the luxury of having fresh venison in the summer, of having an icehouse in which to store fresh meat. She left the quarter hanging, cutting deeply into the chilled flesh with a knife she found there, ringing the thigh bone for two round steaks. The meat smelled wild, like the sage that painted the prairie silver in the sun, like the sage leaves Max had crushed between his fingers a hundred years ago that afternoon and offered to Catherine so that she might sniff their pungency.

This was not the first time Catherine had prepared venison. The master of the Boston home fancied himself a hunter, and when he downed an animal, he offered the carcass to the staff because he didn't fancy the taste.

Catherine carried the steak and a few potatoes back to the dugout where she coated the meat with flour and salt and pepper and shaved the potatoes into thin slices.

There was a bucket of kindling and a box of coal beside the stove. Catherine tossed the kindling into the stove and threw in a scoop of coal. Next, she spooned lard into a frying pan and set it on top. Within moments, the lard was smoking, and Catherine shoveled steak and potatoes into the pan.

There was a cabinet against the wall that held Max's dishes, four mismatched plates, three coffee mugs, an odd assortment of forks, table knives, and spoons, and worn-out sheets he apparently used for tablecloths.

The settings were rough, but no rougher than the table on which they were put, or the two chairs—one new and obviously for Catherine—that were drawn up to it.

By the time she had arranged the table with the kerosene lamp in the middle, the steak and potatoes were done, and then, as though by cue, Max stepped through the dugout's blanket door. He fussed about, washing his face in a panful of cold water carried from the creek, then slicked down his hair and waited for Catherine to call him to the table.

When she did, he sat down and reached for the steak in one single motion.

"Mr. Bass!" Catherine snapped.

Max jerked to a stop. He sat awkwardly, not knowing what he had done wrong, but knowing Catherine wouldn't hesitate to tell him.

"Mr. Bass," Catherine repeated, her voice taking on a superior air, "it is not proper to attack your food without first giving thanks."

"Thank you, ma'am," Max said, reaching again for the steak.

"Mr. Bass, it is not I you thank, but the Lord for His bounty."

"Thank you, Lord," Max said, spearing a hunk of steak with his fork, and drawing it back to his plate.

Catherine's face was livid. "I can see now why you choose to live in a hole in the ground. Your manners are not suited for the company of humankind."

Max mumbled, "Sorry, ma'am" around a mouthful of potatoes. The effect was something less than he might have hoped.

Catherine bowed her head in prayer and crossed herself, then reached for the plate of steak and potatoes.

After he had finished eating, Max settled back in his chair to drink his coffee and pick his teeth with a splinter of wood broken off a piece of kindling.

"Bunkhouse, ma'am."

And when Catherine looked up with a puzzled expression on her face, Max continued. "My manners are suitable for a bunkhouse. You grab in a grub shack or you don't get."

There was a touch of challenge to Max's voice, and when Catherine finished her dinner, he leaned across the table and looked directly into her eyes.

"I'm glad to see that you're a good Catholic. I was counting on that," and when Catherine's face took on an even more quizzical expression, he continued. "You were probably thinking that you would go back into town tomorrow and get the priest to annul the marriage and then skedaddle back to Boston?"

Catherine nodded.

"Well, the priest isn't in Prairie Rose, and he won't be back for another three months. There isn't another priest for a hundred miles, and none of them would give you an annulment unless they talked to me first. So you're married to me, Mrs. Catherine O'Dowd Bass, whether you like it or not."

Catherine drew back her fist to give Max another lesson in Irish ladies' rights, but something in his eyes, his voice, made her hesitate.

"The straight of it," Max continued, "is that you're not leaving tomorrow, or the day after that, or the next week, either."

Catherine's anger boiled over. "I will leave this den of yours tomorrow whether you *allow* me to or not!"

"No!" Max's deep voice cut into Catherine's speech like the butcher knife had cut into the deer's hind quarter before dinner. "No! You will leave when *I* see fit, and that will be a long time coming, longer still if you don't shut your mouth and listen."

Then there was silence, both glowering at each other across the table.

Max began in a low, very controlled voice. "I told you in my letters that I was a rancher and a coal miner. In a sense that is true. I have land and I have coal. The coal you are burning in the stove now was shoveled out of an outcropping on my land just south of here. Sometimes people take a load and give me fifty cents or a dollar. And I've got about thirty head of cattle scattered around the place."

When Catherine started to protest, Max waved her to silence. "I know! That isn't what I told you. I told you I had a big ranch and a coal mine that was selling coal to the railroad. Well, I haven't got that yet, but I will."

Max raised an eyebrow, waiting for Catherine to challenge him, but she didn't, so he continued. "You wouldn't have come if I had told you the truth. I wouldn't want a wife who would have. I need a woman who aims higher than I am right now."

Catherine couldn't hold the bile down anymore. "Finally you make sense. You wouldn't want a wife who could accept you as you are. Well, I can't. So if you will please harness the mare, you and I will be shut of one another."

Max retorted through gritted teeth. "You made it wonderfully clear what you think of me, but for once it is best that you bite that rattlesnake you call a tongue and listen."

They glared at each other, and then Max continued. "This is 'next year' country. Next year, there'll be rain. Next year, we'll have an open winter. Next year, the price of beef will be up. It's always been like that. I came in here with one of the first Texas herds as a kid, and I know that.

"The problem is that most folks sit around waiting for next year to make things better. I've been working on next year for the past twenty years.

"I was a cowhand. Most work all month for nothing more than a hangover. I figured out early on that that's not very smart. So I've been putting my money away for more than twenty years—poker winnings, too. Just a little here and a little there. But I've got money for next year.

"When they opened this land up for homesteading, I said good-bye to the Bar X and rode down here and scouted out this section. It's got water—that's the most precious thing out here—and coal that just pokes out of the ground. Now that ain't worth much yet, but it will be.

"I'm getting things in place for next year. I've got the money, and I've got the land. But none of that means much if you're alone, if you haven't got a home. So I needed you—and lumber for a picket fence and chickens. I never had a home, so maybe I'm not doing this the way I should, but I'm willing to work at it until I get it right."

And when Catherine said nothing, Max continued. "Ma'am, I've spent most of my life on this prairie. I know this land. I know it isn't any more fit for farming than I am. If we get about four dry years in a row, this country will be nothing but dust and busted mortgages.

"I can pick up fifty, sixty sections then. It will be a while before the land heals—they've torn her up so. But she will heal, and then I'll be the rancher I was telling you about in those letters."

"Those are grand plans, Mr. Bass, but when the others go broke, you will, too. You will be in the parade leaving this place. All I'm doing is beating you to it. I'll be wanting a ride to Prairie Rose tomorrow—early."

"Two things," Max said, an edge creeping into his voice. "One, I've got money, a little over five thousand dollars. Never told anybody but you about that. Second thing is that you aren't leaving tomorrow morning. You aren't leaving until the priest comes back in three months, and only then if I say so.

"You ask anybody around here, ma'am. I'm one to soft break a horse, but I break 'em. Never had a horse I couldn't handle."

"A horse!" Catherine hissed. "You are comparing me to a horse! Mr. Bass, I didn't know the true meaning of son of a bitch until I met you. There is only one way to handle someone of your caliber and that is with something of this caliber."

The next moment Max was looking down the barrel of his .44-40 Colt. Damn! He had spent months working on every detail of his plan, but he hadn't counted on her looking into his trunk, finding his pistol, and turning it on him. Who the hell would ever think a woman—a woman from Boston—would get the jump on him like that?

The old pistol's bore looked big as a silver dollar, and it was unwaveringly trained on the bridge of Max's nose. Max was working very hard to appear calm. Was it loaded? He had put it away so long ago, he couldn't remember, and held low the way it was in the shadow under the table, Max couldn't look into the cylinder for the glint of lead. Damn!

Max's mind was racing, trying to find some solution to this mess, but it was coming up empty. "Ma'am, I didn't tell you the whole story. If you will just hold on for a minute. . . ." The hammer went back with an ugly click. Damn! That Colt had a hair trigger. Just bumping it against the table would touch it off. Max's back straightened, and he braced himself for the bullet.

"Ma'am," Max said, the strain poking through his voice. "One of the reasons that I . . . uh . . . lied to you is that I wanted a woman with spirit. I wanted a woman who knew what she wanted and wasn't afraid to go after it. . . ."

"Son of a bitch!"

Max jerked at the sound of Catherine's voice as though it were the tread of the hangman on his gallows.

"What did you think you were doing," she sneered, "buying a horse? Do you think that you had the right to shop for a wife, looking for just the right pedigree to share your den?"

"Ma'am, it wasn't like that. Now you aren't going to use that pistol. I know you aren't the kind of person to pull the trigger. But somebody could be hurt by accident, and I know you wouldn't like that to happen. So maybe you better give it to me, and I'll put it away for you."

Max reached for the pistol, and Catherine pulled the trigger. . . . CLICK!

The click cut off sound and thought and movement, almost as though the pistol had fired, and when Max realized that he wasn't dead, his breath escaped in one long sigh.

"See, it wasn't even loaded," he squeaked. "Uh, just so you don't think I'm trying to pull anything funny, maybe I'd better sleep outside tonight. I'll bed down with the chickens so the coyotes won't bother them."

Max gathered his bedroll in one swoop of his arms and carried it outside. He stopped there, taking deep breaths of the cool night air. A shiver passed over him, and it had nothing to do with the chill moving across the land. He looked up at the stars that calmed him most nights, his problems and aspirations insignificant when measured against heaven's depth and breadth and beauty. But he saw no peace there tonight, only emptiness.

She actually had pulled the trigger. Catherine O'Dowd Bass pointed a pistol at her husband on their wedding night and pulled the trigger. What the hell had he gotten himself into? Max would spend the remainder of the night pondering that question.

CHAPTER 6

MAX awoke with a noseful of chicken. He had bedded next to the wagon, and it fairly reeked with the foul odor. But it wasn't the chickens that had awakened him.

Something in the night had poked into his consciousness, so he lay still, measuring his breath to the natural cadence of a sleeping man. Ever so slowly he opened his eyes. It was always best to know which way to jump before you made a move.

He glimpsed a flicker of movement just at the lip of the slope leading down to Pishkin Creek. Coyote. Must be a coyote after the chickens. No! The two shadowy figures outlined against the horizon were wolves, big prairie wolves. Two at least, maybe others. Strange they would venture so close this time of year. Max watched them for a full two minutes, and they watched him, each unsure of the intentions of the other. Then Max raised his arm, and they disappeared without a sound as though they were nothing more than an early morning dream.

It was early, the stars winking out against a gray sky, but there was little chance of more sleep with all the thoughts bumping around in his head. Max rolled back the bedroll and stood, shivering a little in the early morning chill. He stepped a little away from the wagon to relieve himself. He didn't want any telltale puddle: no telling what that woman would say about that.

Probably wasn't proper to pee near a wagonload of

chickens. Probably a book somewhere that said that proper people don't do that, and no doubt she had read it. She wouldn't hesitate to tell him about her opinion of men who didn't go by the book, either. She was a woman who spoke her mind, no matter how much it stung.

Everything Max did was wrong—by her standards, anyway. He lived in a den, and ate like a hog. The more Max thought about it, the more it grated on his nerves. What made that woman so high and mighty? She was a mail-order bride, not a princess.

And then, as the sun cracked the eastern horizon, Catherine's voice floated up to him from the dugout.

"Mr. Bass!"

The voice seemed out of place. Except for an occasional visitor, an occasional trip to town, Max had spent the last three years alone, the sound of a woman's voice scarce as summer rain.

Max walked over to the edge of the hill and looked down. Catherine was below, fully dressed and standing by the dugout door. At least she was no slugabed.

"Mr. Bass, where is the . . . uh, facility?"

"Ma'am?"

"The toilet."

Max's face lit up. "Just a minute. I should have shown it to you last night, but I wanted you to see it in daylight. Just built it. Had you in mind when I did."

"How nice."

Max continued his running monologue as he led Catherine downstream toward the corral.

"Put it in an arm of the coulee, just before we get to the corral. Close enough to the dugout, but not too close. I built her solid. You'll appreciate that when a blizzard blows through here."

Max slowed as he neared the corral. The trail from

there to the outhouse was faint, not yet worn through the grass that carpeted the coulee bottom.

"There she is, ma'am," Max said, looking back to watch her face as she appraised his handiwork.

The outhouse was well constructed—solid. Each joint in the siding overlapped to ensure that the building would be tight against winter winds and summer flies.

"Got lap cedar roofing, ma'am. Don't see much of that around here, and ma'am," Max said, pausing for effect, "you will be the first."

"Why, Mr. Bass," Catherine said. "You honor me. I don't know if I should go in or christen it with that bottle of champagne your friend gave us."

She laughed then, taking some of the sting from her words, but Max's face was already glowing with dull, red heat.

"Where was the old outhouse?"

"I made do."

Catherine's lip curled. "I'm sure you did. Well, at least when I leave, you will be better off for my having been here. Now please give me some privacy."

Max walked back toward the dugout muttering to himself. That woman sorely tested a man's patience. That outhouse was as fine a piece of handiwork as Max had ever seen, and he had seen more than his share. But was this Boston woman Catherine pleased? Of course not.

By the time Max reached the creek crossing, his anger was at a low boil. Who was this mail-order bride to sneer at him? And worse, why was he still trying to please her? He was acting like a schoolboy, and each time he laid his pride before her, she stepped on it, smeared it with her big-city shoes. There was only so much, by gawd, that a man could take.

When Catherine pulled back the blanket door of the dugout, Max was already inside, turning sizzling salt pork in the pan on the stove. He glanced up at her, and returned to his work, and for some reason, his inattention irked her.

Max waved her to a chair at the table, and then cracked four eggs into the frying pan.

"Oh," Catherine said. "Fresh eggs. Did the chickens lay them?"

"No, ma'am, these are skunk eggs."

Catherine rose to the bait like a trout chasing a caddis fly across a wild stretch of river. "Mr. Bass, your tongue is as dull as your wit."

Max's lips pulled back from his teeth. "I may not be as witty as some of your Boston friends, but I know where chicken eggs come from."

"You, sir, are not as witty as *any* of my Boston friends."

Then, the bitterness vented like an obscene blessing, the two began eating, each raising his or her eyes occasionally to glare at the other. Finally, Max broke the silence. "Have to build a chicken yard today, so I'll be going over on the north side of the ridge to get some posts. Won't take too long. I'd like you to go along."

"I'd like to go back to Prairie Rose."

"Ma'am," Max said, his face contorted with the effort of holding his anger under control, "you are not going back to Prairie Rose until I say you are.

"I told you once that I've never had a horse I couldn't break. Well, you can't break horses if you don't keep them corralled. You, Mrs. Catherine O'Dowd Bass, are corralled. And you will stay that way until I decide that I can no longer tolerate your foul temper and pointed tongue."

When Catherine replied, it was with downcast eyes and a strangely subdued voice. “It is, then, as I feared. I am your prisoner.”

“No, ma’am,” Max said, his anger gone like the air from a punctured balloon. “You are my wife.”

“I see little difference.”

Those words stung more than any she had said in anger. There was soul-withering truth in that simple statement.

Catherine was a prisoner. Max had spent months building a trap for her, examining it from all angles so there was no way for her to wiggle free once entangled.

And then Max baited the snare with lies, carefully chosen to attract a special prey.

Catherine O’Dowd was special. She was ambitious, or she would have stayed in Ireland. She was bright, or she would not have so quickly assimilated the proper speech and manners of the mansion in Boston. She was pretty and would bear Max sons worthy of the empire he would build. But mostly, she was vulnerable, a woman alone in a new land without friends or family to turn to. She was perfect.

And when she came to Prairie Rose, Max slipped the trap, a ring of gold, over her finger. She could not escape that trap. It held her as firmly as spiked jaws hold a bear. Her upbringing would not allow her to pull that ring from her finger no matter how great the pain. Catherine O’Dowd was Max’s prisoner, and he would not let her go.

And now the guilt of that drove him from the table. He paused at the door. “Edna figured out about what your size would be from your picture, and I bought some ranch clothes for you. They’re in the top two drawers of that dresser over there. You should put them on before we go up the hill."

Catherine didn't bother to look up.

"How long, Mr. Bass?"

"Ma'am?"

"I served three years to pay for my ticket to America. How long must I serve to pay you back for my ticket to Montana?"

"Ma'am, it ain't like that at all. I . . . I'll be back as soon as I harness the team."

Max stepped out of the dugout, carrying a wagonload of guilt on his shoulders. He felt as though he had just sobered up from a three-day drunk, and one of his friends had just filled him in on all the sordid details. He didn't feel that he was a bad man, but somehow he had become a villain. He wanted nothing more from life than most men did: a livelihood, a home, and a family. He had done nothing more than was necessary to acquire those things. Was that so terrible?

The horses nickered as Max approached the corral. He filled a bucket with rolled oats, and the Percherons trotted over to him. While the horses were eating, Max draped the harness over their backs, collars over their necks. Then he slipped the bits between their teeth and walked the horses up the hill and backed them to the wagon.

Max took great pleasure in these two giant horses. A simple clucking sound would set more than a ton of muscle leaning into the harness. Little could resist that power. Stumps, rocks, and the breast of the earth yielded to that pure, honest strength. In return, they asked nothing but oats in a box, a soft voice, and an occasional slap on the shoulder.

Max turned the wagon in a wide sweep, letting the

horses get the feel of the harness, and then he drove the team and wagon off the hill toward the creek ford at the bottom. He left the horses waiting there, muscles of a strong right arm tied to Max's will by harness and reins and habit.

One after another Max carried the boxes of chickens to the lean-to where he had wintered that first year. They would be safe there until he and Catherine returned from the ridge with posts to build a chicken yard. Not likely a coyote or wolf would come in broad daylight, and no way a skunk could breach the lean-to and chicken wire, too.

Next came an axe and saw from the tack shed and a promise to pick up the Winchester, even though there wasn't much chance of seeing wolves, much less of getting a shot. Wolves could pick the silhouette of a man out of a jumble of juniper and pine a mile away.

Max walked to the dugout, calling out before entering so as not to surprise Catherine. But when he stepped inside, she was already dressed. She stood beside the dresser in denim pants and a shapeless shirt and heavy shoes.

"Is this suitable?" Catherine asked quietly. "Is this how servant people dress in Montana?"

"Ma'am, I don't want a servant. I want a wife."

"You may force me to be your servant, Mr. Bass, but you will never force me to be your wife."

They stood quietly then, neither looking at the other. Finally, Max said, "Let's go," and Catherine followed him to the door. He paused there long enough to take the rifle from a box near a pile of firewood.

"I never leave it loaded," he said, and then wished he hadn't, but Catherine didn't seem to notice.

They walked downstream to the wagon. Catherine

refused Max's arm and climbed in. The two set off in surly silence. The air was relatively cool, the sun not yet in full control of the day. Light attacked the prairie from the flank, leaving long shadows stretching off toward the west and north. The shadows gave definition to rocks and trees and bushes that would be hidden later in the day.

Catherine had seen the prairie flattened by the brightness of the sun. Now she was seeing the land in better light, sculpted into gentle shapes by heat, rain, and cold. There was beauty on each side, subtle beauty in pastel shades and sweeping curves. Here and there, yucca pointed sharp spines menacingly into the air, warning all creatures to stay clear of its seed pods or suffer the consequences. Tall juniper stood like exclamation points on a page of understatement, and everywhere bunch grass yielded to the passing wagon as the sea yields to a ship.

They followed the gentle contour of the creek until Max clucked the team up the steep lower reaches of a ridge that stretched away to the top of the butte. The ridge top was narrow and the sides were steep, and Catherine reluctantly, and silently, admitted Max's expertise with team and wagon.

The redolent scent of sage below was complemented as they neared the top with the clean, sweet smell of the pine trees. Bull pine lined the upper reaches of each coulee, leading from the sandstone rimrocks above to the prairie below. It was beside one of these stands that Max pulled the wagon to a halt. He climbed down and shook his head when Catherine tried to follow.

"Won't take long. I'll just drop two or three. I can trim them and cut them into posts and have them stacked by the wagon in a few minutes. Got something above that I want to show you."

Max walked through the stand, picking small, dead, and ailing pine. He notched the trees uphill toward the wagon and then cut through the other side, watching with satisfaction as they fell just where he planned.

The trees were small—didn't need much of a post to hold in chickens and hold up chicken wire—and Max's Swede saw ate through them in big bites. He left some of the trees almost full length. These would be poles to line the pen top and sides.

Max carried the posts three at a time up the hill and then returned for the poles, dragging them to the untidy pile beside the wagon.

"Ought to do it," he said, wiping imaginary sweat from his forehead with his shirtsleeve in an old habit. "Now, let me show you something."

Max climbed into the wagon, slapped the reins across the horses' backs, and drove the team up the ridge and out on the flat top of the butte. He climbed down, walked around to Catherine's side of the wagon, and offered her his hand. This time she took it, stepping gracefully down from the wagon seat.

Vegetation was sparse there, soil clinging to the rock only in patches. But wherever there was soil, there was grass and brush. Here and there, trees wedged their roots into cracks in the rock, their stunted size and twisted trunks testaments to their will to live even in that hostile environment.

Walking was easy across that huge, flat rock, and a moment later Max and Catherine were standing at the edge of a cliff on the north side of the butte's narrow waist.

Catherine looked down. The rim fell perhaps eighty

feet to hard-edged rocks below. Suddenly, she felt as though the earth's axis had tipped, and she teetered on the brink. She stood there swaying, until Max took her arm, steadying her.

"Okay?"

"Yes, I don't know what happened."

"Lot farther looking down than it is looking up."

Catherine said softly, "I know that perhaps better than anyone," but Max didn't seem to hear her.

"First thing I did when I came here was to work on those springs and dam up some of those coulees. Then I got the neighbors to chip in, and I built fences while they worked on their homes. Cattle need water nearby, otherwise they walk off weight going from the grass to the water.

"Those first years have paid off. I'm going into winter with fat stock and good grass. Some of the neighbors are already short, and they've got no hay. They stocked too heavy, and didn't pay attention. They're all grazed off close up to water and no way to get to the grass farther out.

"I'll get through the winter, and they might not. Might be that I can pick up some cattle cheap this winter. Maybe some proven homesteads next spring."

"You seem terribly pleased at the prospect of your neighbors' misfortune."

"I know how to live on this land. Some don't."

"Some don't *want* to."

The muscles of Max's jaw tightened. "No market for winter beef," he continued through clenched teeth as they walked toward the southern edge of the rim. "If I don't buy their cattle, the owners will butcher them. But they can't butcher their whole herd, so some drift against a fence, and the wind cuts the life out of them.

"Or they maybe starve down weak, and coyotes get at them. I came up on a bunch of coyotes eating a steer one time. They were having so much fun they didn't even hear me. They had already opened his belly, and two or three were playing tug of war with his guts. One coyote had his head right inside that steer's belly. I don't know what he was chewing on in there, but it was good enough that he didn't even know it when those other coyotes scattered.

"I walked up on that animal same as I would a ranch dog. He heard me just as I got there, and jerked his head out—all bloody, it was. I had him then. He was growling and snapping, but I was so mad I held him by the nape of the neck, and I hoisted him into the air and cut his throat, slow and easy.

"It ain't a kind thing to die like that steer did alone on the prairie. No kind thing at all."

Max stopped a moment to take off his hat and wipe his dry forehead with his shirtsleeve. He didn't look at Catherine. Instead his eyes were fixed on something in the distance.

"*You* try to tell some rancher next winter that he will have to watch his cattle die because you don't want to take unfair advantage of him by giving him money for something that ain't worth spit froze to death. Tell him that while he watches the herd he nursed from calves die, and he can't do nothing to save them. You tell him that, miss high-and-mighty Boston lady, and see how much he's impressed with your neighborliness."

Catherine sagged from the force of Max's words. "I'm sorry."

"You ought to be sorry. Never knew anybody who could learn anything with his mouth open, and near as I can tell, you haven't shut it since you came here."

Catherine's temper flashed.

"Mr. Bass, I am sorry I falsely accused you. You have so many real offenses against you, there is no need to imagine any. And anytime you get tired of me, please feel free to send me back."

"Madam, trains don't go where you came from."

Catherine's eyes narrowed, and her hands knotted into little fists. "Oooooh," Catherine said, poking both fists into the sky, "Lord, give me strength."

Max stepped back.

"No, Mr. Bass, I wasn't going to hit you," she said, the anger turning to exasperation in Catherine's voice. "Go ahead and show me what you want to show me. This place is unbearable."

They walked together to the edge of the rim on the southern side of the butte. They were standing at the base of a shallow U cut back into the sandstone rim, arms stretching south as though to embrace the winter sun.

"See down there, the green? That's a spring. That's where the real ranch is going to be. It faces south and has protection from the wind on the other three sides. It's got water. After I work over that spring, there'll be plenty of water for the house and stock, too."

It was a magnificent homesite. Sandstone cliffs overlooked the little valley. A lifetime would be well spent watching light and shadow play across the face of those rocks. Giant boulders, shaken from the rim by cataclysmic forces or the final drop of centuries of rain and ice, lay imbedded in the valley below. A small stand of trees hugged the rim on the northeast corner, and brush, turning red and yellow in the heat, competed with grass for the water near the spring.

"Why didn't you dig your hole here, Mr. Bass?"

"Soil's too sandy."

"Certainly a nice place for a hole."

Max stared at her for a moment and then sighed. "Neighbors coming day after tomorrow to raise a barn. Wedding present. Give you a chance to get to know some of them."

"I have no desire to meet anyone who holds you in such high esteem as to build a barn for you, and it will be a cold day in hell before I allow anyone to see me in that snake pit you call home."

"Ma'am, I've weathered storms that froze cattle standing straight up, and I've never seen anything as cold as this place has been the past couple of days."

"Maybe hell *has* frozen over, Mr. Bass. This certainly is as close as I ever want to come."

Max sighed again.

"I have to go to town today to order the lumber. You're welcome to go along."

"You want me to be seen in public dressed like this?"

"I'm going dressed like *this,*" Max said.

Catherine's lip curled.

"Stop at the dugout. I'll change."

The ride to town was silent save for the creak and rattle of the wagon and the clapping of the horses' hooves against the prairie hardpan.

Catherine's mind was racing. She might escape, but how? She had no money, her savings spent in Boston because she knew she was marrying a rich Montana rancher and wouldn't need the few coins in her cloth bag. But now she desperately needed money, enough for a ticket to somewhere else, someplace Max wouldn't find her.

These same thoughts were bumping through Max's

mind, but reversed as by a mirror. Catherine might—probably would—run, but only if he turned his back. Her pride was too fragile to bump it against the eyes and wagging tongues of the people of Prairie Rose.

So on they rode in silence, each plotting against the other.

Max pulled the mare up to the hitching post outside Cole's General Store and climbed down, stepping to the other side of the wagon to give Catherine his hand. "Might as well come in."

"I thought I would go over to the dry goods store."

"There'll be time for that later."

They went in together. The store smelled of leather, vegetables, tin, spices, floor oil, tobacco, horses, and a blend of other odors too exotic or intertwined to recognize.

A tobacco rope, woven of half-inch strands of leaf, hung by the door, and a long glass-front counter ranged the length of the building. Shelves lined the walls floor-to-ceiling, and stepladders offered access to their shadowed depths. Goods hung on ropes spun down from the high tin-clad ceiling like spider webs to trap customers with their wares, and the aisle wended its way through a maze of saddles, farm gear, sacks of potatoes, and whatever else needed immediate space.

Catherine had never seen a store like it. She wandered, drawn finally to a shelf full of hats. Pastel green and beautiful it was, and capped with a bouquet of silk flowers.

Mrs. Cole, two axe handles high and one wide, appeared behind the counter. "It's the green one, isn't it?"

Catherine was startled by the woman's intrusion.

"No, I mean yes, but I don't need a hat."

"Thought so. The green will bring out the color of your eyes. You must try it on."

"No, I . . ."

Mrs. Cole bustled around the end of the counter, and reached almost full length to place the hat on Catherine. She stepped back, head cocked, surveying her handiwork, then leaned into Catherine again, tipping the hat just a bit over one eye.

"Thought so," she said. "That hat's been here for a year now, and there hasn't been one lady to come in but doesn't try it on. Just wasn't right for any of them, but on you it looks like a crown. Matches your dress, too. You could wear it home."

"But I . . ."

"Here, the mirror."

Even in the pale light, Catherine knew Mrs. Cole was right. The hat drew attention to her eyes, to the color of her skin. And then in the mirror, Catherine noticed that Max was watching her, the same look on his face as that first day when he saw her swinging beside the creek. Catherine blushed.

"Put the hat on the ticket with the lumber," Max said without taking his eyes from Catherine. George Cole, who had interrupted taking Max's order to watch the affair, smiled, and then fidgeted.

"Uh . . . there's something that we have to talk about, Max."

Max turned his attention to the storekeeper.

"I can't put the lumber or the hat on a ticket for you." Cole pulled a dust rag from his back pocket and ran it across the countertop. Polishing the glass seemed to take his full attention, and he spent some time at it before continuing. "Fact is, Max, I can't give you any credit."

Max bristled. "You can't give me credit?"

Cole shook his head.

"You owe *me* money for this year's wheat, don't you?"

Cole nodded.

"Then what the hell do you mean you can't give *me* credit?"

Cole sucked in a long breath. "The fact is Max, that the banker told me not to. If I give you credit, I lose mine. I need bank money to operate. Sorry, but that's the way it is."

Max glowered for a moment and then softened. "Sorry, George, should have known it wasn't you. Give Miss Catherine that hat, and make arrangements to deliver the lumber day after tomorrow—Thomsen said he would get some men together to haul it out—and I'll go get the banker his cash money."

Max strode stiff-legged to the door. Credit is a public rating of a man's honesty and dependability. Word might spread that Max Bass was no longer considered good for his debts, and that realization stung. He was thinking about that, and not Catherine, as he left the store.

Catherine counted to thirty and then walked over to the storefront window. Max was just stepping through the door into Millard's. Catherine turned to Mrs. Cole.

"The hat is lovely. I'll take it. If Mr. Bass returns before I do, perhaps you could tell him that I just stepped out for a moment."

Mrs. Cole nodded. "I knew you were right for that hat," she said. "As soon as you stepped through the door. I knew it."

Catherine tugged open the heavy door and sneaked across the boardwalk and into the street. She caught herself then, took a deep breath, and marched the remaining way to the Prairie Rose Bank like a queen about to review her troops.

A bell rang above the door as she entered the bank, and Phillips looked up and blanched. It was that crazy woman with the hat pin, and she was descending upon him again.

"I would like to see you in your office, Mr. Phelps."

"Phillips, ma'am. My name is Phillips."

"No matter. I want to see you in your office."

They marched lockstep into the banker's inner sanctum, and Catherine quietly shut the door behind her. The office was plain and small: one wall mostly taken up by a rolltop desk that didn't have a scrap of paper on it. Phillips motioned Catherine to one of the straight-backed wooden chairs flanking the door and settled his bulk into a padded chair by the desk.

"I would like to withdraw two hundred dollars from Mr. Bass's account."

The banker looked at her speculatively and said, "I'm sure you would. But the fact is, ma'am, that your husband does not have an account in this bank. You might say he is 'no account.' "

The banker erupted into wheezing chuckles that concluded in a fit of coughing.

"You might say that, Mr. Phelps, but I am not that lacking in intellect."

Phillips choked off his laughter. "You're pretty high and mighty for a woman who lives in a hole."

"Compared to you, Mr. Phelps, nearly everyone must seem high and mighty."

Phillips's right eyelid began to twitch, and his pasty face took on a pinkish hue.

"Madam, I am president of the Prairie Rose Bank. I

am responsible for thousands of dollars deposited here. You will treat me with the respect I deserve."

"If I gave you the respect you deserve, I would likely be arrested for assault and battery. You wear this office like a cardboard crown, but like you, it has no substance. It would take an act of God, sir, to make a man of you."

"*Madam,*" Phillips said, wringing sarcasm from the word as one might wring dishwater from a rag. "I was not the one so desperate for a husband that I ran all the way from the East Coast to marry a penniless man who lives in a cave."

That blow struck home, and Catherine flinched. When she spoke, she was quiet, subdued.

"Perhaps I have no more substance than you, Mr. Phelps, but whatever else Maxwell Bass is, he is a self-made man, not a chameleon like you who takes on the color of his surroundings. And he is hardly penniless. I would guess that the five thousand dollars he has hidden on his ranch is far more than you have hidden in this bank."

"So that's what you're after," the banker said, reflection replacing the heat of a moment ago. "Max has managed to put away some money, and you're after it. I wondered what led a pretty woman like you to marry a man like Bass. So . . . you're a whore, after all, aren't you Catherine Bass?"

Catherine's face bleached white, and then turned a dull heated red. The banker could feel that heat, and his eyes widened as she reached to her new green hat and pulled the pin from it.

The banker Phillips sat alone, immersed in pain. That bitch had poked him again. He would take great pleasure in wreaking revenge on Bass and his crazy wife. And now he had the key.

Bass had five thousand dollars stashed on the ranch, and he had as much as stolen that much and more from the banker. If Bass hadn't ruined the banker's oil swindle, Phillips would be lying on the beaches of Southern France by now, a lady on each arm. All the banker intended was to collect what Bass owed him.

It wasn't like stealing the money. Not really. Bass probably stole it from someone else, anyway. No way a cowpoke like him could put together that much money honestly. And so Bass wouldn't be able to report the theft—appropriation—when he realized his money was gone.

It wouldn't be hard to find, either. Man like Bass would pick an obvious place to hide it and would probably check on it now and again just to be sure. Watch him for a few days, and he'd point the way.

A grin began to widen the corners of the banker's mouth. It was time to write cousin Milburn, but first he'd take a run out to Max's himself. Maybe he wouldn't need any help. No sense splitting a pot when you could have it all for yourself.

The ride back to the dugout for Max and Catherine was as silent as the trip to Prairie Rose. This time they were thinking about the banker Phillips, but for completely different reasons.

CHAPTER 7

THE double tub was perched on four piles of flat rock beside the creek: beneath a fire raged, sparks riding smoke into the morning air. Max watched the flames, and occasionally pitched another log on the fire.

He looked up as Catherine stepped from the dugout, trying to read her mood from the way she walked, but it was probably best that he couldn't.

Catherine was hoping Max would have at least a crick in his back or red eyes from another night spent on the ground beside the wagon, but he didn't seem any the worse for it. That was mildly exasperating, like swinging a newspaper at a fly—and missing.

As Catherine neared, Max spoke. "Won't be long," he said, nodding toward the tub.

"Mr. Bass, if you think I'm going to take a bath out here, you are sadly mistaken."

Max looked at Catherine as though she were an insect he had not seen before, interesting, but not something he would like to know on a personal level.

"It's for the chickens," he said.

"You're going to give the chickens a bath?"

"You really don't know, do you?"

"Know what?"

"How to butcher chickens."

"It is not high on my list of priorities."

"It is about to be, as soon as this water starts boiling."

"Well, you watch your pot, Mr. Bass, until it boils, and

I will be back in a few moments. I wouldn't miss this for the world, entertainment being so scarce out here."

"You'll see it all right," Max muttered as Catherine walked down the path to the privy. "You're going to play a starring role in it."

The morning was glorious, blue sky stretching from horizon to horizon without blemish, and just a hint of chill in the air, an omen of coming fall.

Max greeted the changing of the seasons with great expectation. The heat of the summer was welcome until he wilted under it. Fall was magic—cool, bright days, and nights so clear he could almost read by starlight—but given time, fall turned from reds and golds and blues to browns and grays. He gloried in the first snowfall, as nature wiped her canvas clean, scrubbing off faded colors of earlier seasons. But when the cold, that long unforgiving, unrelenting cold, held all creatures in thrall, Max would long for the pale greens and bright flowers of spring. He awaited each change, tired of what had been, eager for what would be.

When Catherine returned, Max had a fire blazing in the stove and a healthy portion of sidepork sizzling in a pan. He speared the finished slices with a fork, stacking them on a waiting plate. Then he dropped little slabs of bread dough he had made the night before into the hot grease.

The grease sputtered, crackled, and boiled, and it was only a few moments before the bread was golden brown. Max shoveled the finished product on a plate and dropped more dough into the frying pan. He motioned for Catherine to sit and brought the sidepork and fried bread over to the table.

"What is that?" Catherine asked, pointing at the plate of bread.

"Not proper to point," Max said, immediately wishing he hadn't. He didn't want to fight anymore. He was tired of the anger and sharp words. He desperately wanted this day to be better than the last. When Catherine didn't retaliate, Max breathed a quiet sigh of relief.

Catherine watched Max cut a slab of butter and smear it over the top of the hot bread. Then he sprinkled sugar on it and ate. Catherine followed his lead. It was good, very good.

"What is this?"

"Indians call it fry bread. Scandihoovians call it dough-de-dads."

"What do you call it?"

"Well, if I'm with Indians, I call it fry bread, and if I'm with the Scandihoovians, I call it dough-de-dads."

"How original," Catherine said lightly. The insult was simply habit. She didn't want to fight any more than Max did. "It's good."

"Thank you."

That civil exchange surprised them both. They raised their eyes for a moment, each to look at the other, and quickly returned their attention to their plates, shy without the anger that had defined their relationship over the past few days.

"I would appreciate a little help with the chickens this morning," he said.

"I'll check my social calendar, but if I'm free, I would be happy to lend a hand."

It was Catherine's first attempt at humor with Max, and he approached it warily, as a coyote approaches the bait in a trap.

"Thank you."

"You're welcome."

Catherine rose and began gathering the dishes, but Max interrupted her.

"I'll do that. Nothing to it, just a few dishes. You go outside. It's a pretty morning."

Catherine nodded, walking toward the door. Each spent the next ten minutes wondering what the other was up to.

When Catherine returned from her brief walk up the creek, Max was carrying a log and a double-bitted axe. He stood the knee-high section of log on one end and laid the axe beside it. He was stirring the fire as Catherine approached.

"Be a great help if you would catch some chickens for me," Max said.

When Catherine nodded, he handed her a single strand of heavy fencing wire bent at one end into a narrow V.

Catherine took the wire, trying not to appear as confused as she felt. She turned to walk to the chicken pen and then stopped.

"Mr. Bass, I must admit that I don't know what to do with this wire."

Max took the wire from her and walked to a small stand of willows by the creek. "It's to catch the chickens. Just slip the wire past a chicken's leg and pull back, like this," he said, catching a willow in the V.

"Of course," Catherine said, her confidence returning. She walked to the pen where the chickens were contentedly scratching in patches of dust for the grain Max had thrown that morning. As she neared the gate, the chickens flocked to her, expecting more grain. Catherine tried to shoo them away, but the birds held fast, conditioned to believe that man—or woman—held more promise than threat.

Catherine unlatched the gate, forcing her leg into the opening to block the chickens from escaping while she entered the pen. But one hen, spying a loose thread on her cuff, reached out and pecked it. Catherine squealed and withdrew her leg, and the other birds took that as an invitation and began crowding through the gate. Before Catherine regained control, there were ten to fifteen hens around the creek bottom, hell bent for elsewhere.

Catherine shrieked and charged into the nearest knot of birds, waving the wire Max had given her like a foil. The chickens squawked and ran from the strange creature.

Catherine screeched and followed.

Max leaned back as one hen sped past, desperately trying to fly, Catherine in hot pursuit. The bird was touching ground only every third or fourth step and might have eventually become airborne, had the creek not interrupted its takeoff. *Splash!* The bird fluttered about halfway across before plunging into the water. Catherine tried to stop short on the bank, but her feet slipped on the mud, and her legs shot straight out in front of her. *Splash!*

"Thought you weren't going to take a bath," Max said, immediately wishing he hadn't.

"What," Catherine sputtered, "did you say?"

"Said your chicken is drowning."

The chicken, indeed, appeared to be in trouble. It was being swept along in the creek swimming first one way and then the other.

Catherine leaped into pursuit, chasing the bird down the creek, silver splashes marking each step. She fell again, this time head first and full length. When she came up she was shaking her head, spray flying from her hair. Clutched to her breast was the chicken.

"Got her," she said triumphantly.

Catherine struggled back to Max, holding the chicken to her and petting its head.

"Easier to catch the chickens *inside* the pen," Max said. Catherine's eyes flashed cold and hot at the same time.

"Easy to sit here and make smart remarks while I do all the work."

"I'll trade jobs if you want."

"And just what are you doing, Mr. Bass?"

"Here, I'll show you."

Max took the chicken from Catherine's arms, holding both the bird's legs in his left hand. Upside down, the bird quieted and Max laid its head and neck on the log.

Thunk! The double-bitted axe passed through the neck of the chicken and stuck in the log. The chicken tried one last time to fly, wings beating wildly as Max threw the carcass on the ground. Catherine watched in horrified fascination as the head, still lying on top of the log, continued to move as though the hen were trying to squawk its indignation.

It was then that Max noticed that Catherine's plunge in the creek had left her clothes wet and clinging, and when she felt Max's eyes on her body, the gold flecks in her eyes flashed again.

"Mr. Bass, it is best that you keep your mind on your chickens. You have, at least, some hope of catching *them*."

Max's face was burning again. Three times he had blushed since meeting Catherine, the only times in his life. This woman had an uncanny ability to put him on the defensive, to make him feel small.

"I'll be back after I change. I believe I have the knack of it."

Catherine marched toward the dugout as though she were leading a parade, leaving Max to his contemplations. What magic did that woman have? In the blink of an eye, or rather an ill-placed stare, Catherine had transformed herself from an inept chicken catcher to Max's moral superior. How did she do that to him?

The next morning, Max rose well before dawn, stars still bright in the sky. He picked up his bedroll, policing the area around the wagon with his eyes. Wouldn't do to leave anything lying about. Max didn't want anyone to know about his sleeping arrangements with his bride.

He was greeted at the dugout by the smell of frying chicken. Catherine had already begun her day. Max paused at the door. He would have knocked had there been anything to knock on, but there wasn't. Instead, he said, "Ma'am?"

"Come in, Mr. Bass. I am quite decent."

Catherine had risen early. She couldn't sleep. Each time she shut her eyes, she saw Max's axe falling and another chicken beating out its protest with a flurry of dead wings.

Most of the chickens had drifted back to the pen after Catherine scattered feed on the ground, food more important than freedom. As they scratched about greedily racing to get more than their neighbors, Catherine had come up behind, snaring one after another and hauling them to Max's axe.

All the chickens died hard. One ran after Max dropped her, faster than she probably had ever run in life. Headless, blind and half-dead she ran, blood spraying from her neck until her heart pumped dry, and death could be ignored no longer.

After the chickens were bled out, Max threw them into the boiling water, scalding them until they could be plucked clean of feathers. Then Max and Catherine dressed the chickens, reaching deep into the birds' body cavities to pull their guts out on a twice-read copy of the *Prairie Rose Printer.* They sifted through the guts dividing hearts, livers, gizzards, and fully-developed eggs. Afterward, Max threw the guts on the fire like an offering to some pagan god, lover of chicken guts.

But the action was purely practical, not spiritual. It would make no sense to let wolves and coyotes and skunks come to associate the Bass Ranch with an easy meal.

Catherine had risen early, cut up the carcasses, shaken the pieces in a mixture of flour and pepper and salt, and tossed them into grease, already sizzling in Max's three big frying pans.

Max stepped through the dugout door, leaving his hat on the pile of wood at the entry. Catherine motioned him to the table. She had fried sidepork for the grease and made dough-de-dads with the last remaining dough kept overnight in a pan covered with a damp towel. They were still warm when Max sat down.

"You're early."

"Didn't want to do any cooking after the other ladies arrive. Don't want anyone to see me in this . . . this," Catherine said, a sweep of her head taking in the dugout.

She had dismissed with that nod all the days Max had spent with a pick and shovel carving the dugout from the bank of clay. He had moved a houseful of dirt from the hillside, hauling it upstream to a narrow stretch of the creek, using earth and logs hauled down from the hill to build a low earthen dam there.

The work had not come easy for Max. The first tasks he had put himself to on the homestead—fencing, developing springs, and damming coulees—had all been respectable work for a cowhand, and bone deep that was what Max was.

But digging the dugout was another matter. Cowhands do not stoop to such labor, considering themselves a breed apart from those who build calluses to fit the handles of shovels and picks. Their souls are better fitted to horizons that stretch wide as the sea than to the confining gray walls of a dugout.

Max had done the work, understanding that it represented a major shift in the direction of his life, and when he was done, he was pleased that he had done it well. That was the credo upon which he had built his life.

And now Catherine sneered at the dugout as she had sneered at the privy, at his dream of building a ranch to fit the breadth of this land.

Catherine had measured Max and found him terribly wanting, and Max was forced for the first time in his life to look at himself by standards more stringent than how well he strung fence or branded calves or played poker. And he was beginning to doubt himself, to see the dirt beneath his fingernails rather than the strength of his hands.

He watched Catherine as he ate, taking care not to be caught with his eyes upon her. She had been beautiful two days ago in Prairie Rose. Standing over the stove, now, dressed in pants and a long-sleeved shirt, hair aflutter and face flushed with the heat, she was more beautiful still.

But to Max, she was like the delicate pink wild rose that traces the waterways of Montana: beautiful, sweet scented, but guarded by a jungle of needle-sharp thorns. And talking to her was like wading into that jungle, knowing there would be thorns to pick from his flesh before he found his way out of the tangle.

But Max wanted to talk, to meld Catherine's time with his own, and he wanted an answer to a question that had been needling him.

"Saw Phillips last night."

Catherine stiffened. She wasn't ashamed of her battle with the banker. He had it coming. But in the heat of the battle, she had betrayed Max's confidence about the money he had hidden on the homestead and made him vulnerable to that despicable man. She felt like a Judas.

Max continued, "Horses nickered, and I walked down along the creek by the corral. There was the banker, digging a hole. I watched him for a minute or two and then came up quiet behind him and asked him what he was doing. He jumped straight up about three rails high. Said he was going fishing. Not too many people go fishing in the middle of the night without a pole, but he said that was the way he liked to do it. Said he could cut himself a willow. He didn't have a can, so I asked him where he kept the worms. He kind of hemmed and hawed and said he always carried them in his pockets to keep them warm. So I helped him pick worms until his pockets were pretty well filled. Didn't even say thank you, just started off downstream like a little kid who had had an accident in his pants, and he walked right past a patch of willows without stopping to cut a pole. Might be he decided he really didn't want to go fishing, after all."

Max looked at Catherine, but she avoided his eyes.

Her fight with Max was personal, and she had shared it with a man who would use it to hurt Max if he could. She felt shame for what she had done and anger at Max for having put her in such an untenable position.

But just as she was about to speak, she was saved by the rumble of wagons and Jake Thomsen's high, clear voice. "Max, about time you got out of bed. We came out here to get some work done, not to sit here getting splinters in our behinds."

Max grinned a little despite himself. Jake and a couple of others from town had arrived early with the lumber he had ordered.

When he glanced back at Catherine, she was rigid by the stove. "Don't you bring them in here," she said, her voice brittle as shore ice in winter.

"They've been in here before."

"Not with me."

"No, not with you." But then neither have I, Max thought, except for a few moments around the table in strained silence or in heated battle. "They'll be expecting breakfast."

"We don't always get what we expect."

"We sure as hell don't."

Catherine's eyes sliced into Max's. "Mr. Bass, that language is probably acceptable to your friends. It is not acceptable to me."

"If you find something that is acceptable to you, I would be obliged if you would let me know. I'd rope it off and sell tickets to it as the eighth wonder of the world."

Catherine looked at Max out of the corner of her eye. "Sometimes you surprise me, Mr. Bass. Somewhere behind that plate of bone you call a forehead, there lurks a light, a dim, dim light, but a light nonetheless."

Max sighed. "These are my friends. Please be nice to them. It is just one day, and then they will be gone."

"You do, then, allow *some* people to leave this . . . palace of yours?"

Max's voice edged sideways through gritted teeth. "Damn it, woman, don't you ever stop?"

"If I trouble you, please feel free to send me on my way."

"I don't want to talk about that now."

"I do. I want your friends to know what kind of a man you really are. Do you think, then, that they would come to this place and build a barn in your honor?"

"Whose part do you think they will take?" Max spat. "They were all standing there at the Patchucks' when you promised to take me for better or worse. You want them to know what an easy liar you are?"

Catherine gasped. In a flash, she was standing by Max's chair, her fork—the only weapon she had—describing a vicious arc toward his face.

Max caught Catherine's wrist, and the two were still struggling as Jake Thomsen poked his head through the door.

"Max, you still in bed?" Jake's grin faded as he saw the two. "Sorry," he said, ducking out the door.

Catherine's voice was like a late fall wind keening through the naked limbs of cottonwoods, reaching in supplication toward an unpromising sky.

"Mr. Thomsen, you said you would help if I needed it. I need it. Please take me to Prairie Rose. Please take me away from this, please . . . please."

Thomsen pretended he hadn't heard her, trying to carry the smile he had taken to the dugout back to the wagon, but it was too heavy a burden.

Max stumbled for the door, taking a deep breath

before plunging through. He appeared outside as though surfacing from the depths of a pool, gasping for air. Max tried to grin, but the effort twisted his face into a macabre mask.

"Miss Catherine is frying chicken. You boys will have to wait on your breakfast," he said, his voice little more than a croak.

And Catherine stood at the stove watching the frying chicken through a veil of tears, as though from behind a rain-streaked window. She would escape this place. One way or another, she would escape.

CHAPTER 8

MAX and Edna Lenington stood silent, unmoving as though by some magic they were taking root, becoming the second and third parts of a cottonwood grove on the creek bottom.

It was full light now, and most of the men were laying the barn's foundation downstream where a flat, bare slab of sandstone overlooked Max's natural corral. The foundation was taking shape, a rough rectangle built of sandstone hauled from an outcropping below.

The families had come just after the sun set fire to the day, children poking solemnly from the beds of slow-moving wagons like sentinel gophers. Once the wagons stopped, the children spilled over the sides and flowed to the creek as naturally as rainwater, sometimes quiet as a meadow brook and sometimes raucous as a mountain torrent, but always to the creek.

The children knew the importance of water instinctively. It was hammered into their subconscious by murmured conversations of their parents, desperate eyes seeking dark clouds.

Consciously, they knew that a creek, open water, would be as close to a carnival as most of them would ever come. Creek water was cool on feet that went dry except for second- or third-hand bathwater on Saturday nights. It was a strange environment inhabited by soft-skinned frogs and snakes that didn't bite and fish that did. And the stream was edged with grass, green and soft, not hard and brittle like August bunch grass.

None of the children could resist the creek: None of them tried.

A barn raising was a holiday, but not from the labor that hardened the homesteaders' hands and stiffened their backs. They would work as hard today as they did at home, harder perhaps, pitting themselves against one another in unannounced contests of skill and strength.

But the day was special. They would share scarce gossip, tap into the rich vein of kinship felt by those who shared life on the Montana prairie. They would tease underused muscles into grins and guffaws and share pieces of their lonely lives with others of their kind.

The men were already at work, following a few quick instructions from Max.

But wives and older daughters stood rooted in the creek bottom with Max and Edna, awaiting the resolution of a breach of prairie etiquette. Catherine was hostess, and she should have been outside to greet the women as they came, to tell them what they needed to know to prepare the day's feast, but still she had not emerged from the dugout. None of them were willing to step in, awed yet by the dignity with which she carried herself at the wedding.

So they fidgeted, watching the doorway of the dugout, awaiting some signal from Catherine.

Signal, they got.

Catherine swept aside the dugout's blanket door and stepped out, pausing a moment for effect. She was wearing a beautiful blue dress, a copy of one she had seen in Boston. It had taken her months to save enough money to buy the material for the dress and weeks to make it, stitching each detail from memory.

She had sewed in secret, knowing that the other servants would laugh at her for believing she would ever have occasion to wear such a dress. But as Catherine sewed, she dreamed of the stir the dress would create among young gentlemen admirers. And today, she glided down the steps from the dugout as though she were leaving the veranda of a Southern mansion to mix with guests on the lawn.

Much to Max's relief, when Catherine spoke she was the model of civility.

"Mrs. Lenington, I'm glad you could come." Then Catherine turned to Max, her smile cold as the moon on a winter night. "Mr. Bass, I thought you would take it upon yourself to set up a table down here in the shade of the cottonwood tree."

Max scurried off.

"Mrs. Lenington, perhaps you wouldn't mind helping me carry the chicken and potato salad to the table?"

Edna nodded and then called to the waiting women. "Table will be here, might as well bring down the food." The women exploded into a rush of talk, walking back to their wagons, eager to get to work.

One said in a stage whisper as she walked away, "Certainly dresses well for a woman who lives in a hole in the ground."

But the woman's companion brought her up short. "Not all of us can live in a nice tarpaper shack like you do, Lucille," and that ended the discussion.

The men had framed the barn's walls on the ground and had them up well before noon. Meanwhile another crew was working on the trusses for the roof. After the walls went up, the trusses were hoisted into place. Then one crew went to work flooring the loft, and others divided up to side the building.

The men swarmed over the emerging barn like ants, moving under the direction of some central intellect or instinct. No one really seemed to be in charge, although occasionally one man or another would approach Max, ask him a brief question, and then return to the barn. His coworkers would gather for a moment and then go back to their tasks with renewed fervor.

Catherine watched, fascinated, until the shade and Edna called her back to the long tables set up along the creek. She found that she was enjoying herself as the day wore on. The shade of the great cottonwood was filled with the buzz of conversation, and hungry women and giggling children.

The Sunday supper was ready. The children, of course, had already been picking at the goodies on the table, snatching a piece of chicken whenever opportunity presented itself. There was much to-do made about these raids with stern looks for the children and grins for the other grown-ups.

The work had been steady since first light, the crew pausing only for long draughts of water hauled in buckets to the barn. The men, women, and children were hungry, but Max didn't want to break for supper until the barn was substantially finished. Once the men had cleared the heavily laden tables and tapped the keg of beer cooling in the creek, work would be swallowed in a vortex of beer and talk and horseshoes.

The tables were covered to protect the food from the flies that gathered for the feast. Catherine, wishing she had worn pants rather than a dress, settled on a rock by the creek when she would have preferred sprawling on the cool grass.

A moment later Edna settled beside Catherine. They sat quietly for a moment, enjoying the shade and the sounds of the creek and the children's laughter.

Catherine had been watching one child about four—too old for his mother's skirts and too young for the rough and tumble play of the older children—hanging about the periphery of the mob that swirled around the creek bottom like a flock of drably colored birds.

The boy was dressed as most of the children were, in cast-off clothes from older children, patched and pinned, held together more from habit than anything. He was easy to pick out from the crowd, and not simply because his hair shown like a shock of wheat in the sinking summer sun. The boy wasn't part of the play, but he seemed determined to do each of the things the others did, to prove to himself, at least, that he was *capable* of playing with others, given the chance.

And more than once the boy's determination had caused Catherine to catch her breath. There was a rock wall on the other side of the creek, thick and slick with summer moss. The older children, amid shrieks and dares, had edged each in turn out on a narrow ledge on that wall, grasping for handholds and footholds that would take them across without falling into the creek below.

The creek ran deep and swift under the ledge, and most of the prairie children didn't know how to swim, never having been around a large enough accumulation of water at any one time to learn. So crossing the ledge was dangerous for the older children, and much more so for the towhead.

But after the other children had passed their test of courage and agility and gone on to other things, the little boy crept out on the ledge. Catherine held her breath as he inched along to the point where the ledge had broken long ago, leaving a thirty-inch gap. He stopped there as the other children had, gauging whether he could step that far while hanging from the only handhold available above him.

And then he stepped. His foot missed the other side by inches, and instantly he was hanging by one hand over the water below, feet scrambling for purchase.

Catherine was too shocked to move, to speak. She sat helplessly, watching the drama played out on that tiny stage. Still he scrambled, his arm stretched tight and thin. It was then that Catherine realized the boy wasn't trying to find his way back to the ledge where he had been standing. He was trying to inch across.

Just as Catherine's lips were forming No! the boy found footing and made his way to the other side. Through it all, only Catherine watched. Everyone else was busy with work that needed doing, saying words that needed saying.

And then Edna took Catherine's attention away from the little boy. "Thought Max would have been over by now to pick up the horses."

"Horses?"

Edna clapped a hand over her mouth. "Lordy, I'm sorry. I guess he wanted to surprise you, and now I've let the cat out of the bag. Honest, I didn't mean to. You won't tell him, will you?"

"I'm sorry, Mrs. Lenington . . ."

"Edna, call me Edna."

"Edna . . . I don't know what you are talking about."

Edna hesitated, and then continued. "Not long after we came—Max had already been here more than a year—Max disappeared early one spring. Didn't tell anyone where he was going or how long he would be gone.

"Came back about a month and a half later, riding the most beautiful horse I'd ever seen. Kind of gray, he is, and white across the rump with spots. Max calls him an appie, picked him up someplace out in Idaho.

"Anyway, right after you agreed to come out here, Max disappeared again, only this time not so long. Guess he had the herd spotted by then, and back he comes with a three-year-old filly, maybe prettier than the stud.

"I swear those horses are smarter than most folks, seem almost able to read your mind sometimes. Max says he's going to build a herd of the best horses in Montana."

"What does that have to do with me?" Catherine asked, a quizzical expression on her face.

It was Edna's turn to look perplexed. "Everything Max does affects you, and the mare is to be yours. Max has already bred it to the stud. Should foal next spring."

"The mare is mine?"

"That's what Max said."

Catherine's jaw jutted into the conversation. "Then, who the hell does he think he is to breed my horse without permission?"

"Well, I don't know," Edna said, taken aback by the drift in the conversation. "I guess you'll have to talk to Max about that."

"No! Max will have to talk to *me* about that."

Edna was in a quandary. She respected Max more than most men, and she had helped him bring Catherine to Montana. She wouldn't intentionally embarrass him or endanger the union for the world.

Still, gossip was as scarce as people on the plains of

eastern Montana. It was passed about with such enthusiasm that it often made two or three rounds—with a few additions and deletions here and there—before it wore out. Edna sensed a bit of real gossip here, and she was torn between her loyalty to Max and her need to dig it out for future reference. Edna was still pondering that dilemma when Catherine poked into Edna's thoughts.

"Whatever in the world are those children doing?"

The children were gathered two deep in a circle on the creek bottom, boys reaching in with sticks, bedeviling some creature in the center.

At first, Catherine thought it was a child's game, with the person "it" in the middle, but the circle was too rigid and there was too little movement inside. And then the game changed. The little towheaded boy broke through the ring and edged into the circle, leading with his right leg, stamping it ahead of him. The children shrieked and hands flew to their faces. A moment later, the boy ran from the circle. Then the children goaded him on, and he entered the circle again, *thump, thump, thump,* and run.

Catherine turned to Edna, who was already rising, distraught.

"Little Zeb, get that boy away," she shouted. She ran toward the children. Catherine followed, embarrassed because she didn't know why she was running or where, because she didn't know whether it was ladylike to run.

Edna reached the towheaded boy just as he started into the circle again, *thump, thump* . . . Edna caught him by the shirt collar and jerked him backward. He struggled there a moment like a fish on a line, but Edna had already turned her attention to the other children.

"I'm ashamed of you!" she said. "You know better!"

"He wanted to, Ma."

But Edna cut through that argument as conclusively as the axe cut short the lives of chickens the day before.

"You wanted to jump off our house to see if you could fly, remember that? What do you suppose would have happened if I had let you do that?"

"I'm sorry, Ma."

"You should be. Little Joey doesn't have anyone to watch him, and you all egged him on to do this. You ought to be ashamed of yourselves!"

Then, snatching a stick from one of the children, she shouted, "Now, all of you kids git!"

And still Catherine didn't know what had upset Edna, not until Edna took the stick and advanced like an avenging angel toward the center of the circle.

And then Catherine knew.

There was a rattlesnake coiled there. Catherine had never seen one, but she knew this was a rattlesnake more certainly than she knew she was her mother's daughter.

Coils topped by an ugly S held its head back, ready to strike. Yellow eyes halved by black, impenetrable slits were untouched by the crush and flow of life on the creek bottom. This was a creature of death, not life, and it awaited Edna, its tail singing its own death song, anxious to kill one more time before it died.

Catherine shuddered, and Edna waded in. She wielded the rod like the angel Gabriel, the stick whistling through the air to land with a *thump.* The rattler was writhing, striking blindly at shadows and weeds and the injustice of having been born with scales and rattles and fangs.

And even after it was over; even after one of the boys had stepped out of the knot of watching children and cut the snake's head off with his pocketknife; even after another boy stepped forward and pulled the rattles, sticking them into his hatband; even after the snake's head was buried so that none of the children would step barefoot on it and inject themselves with poison; still the snake writhed out its indignation.

Catherine was fascinated. Never had she seen anything so ugly and so compelling at the same time.

"They do that till sundown, then they stop," Edna said, a shudder running through her. "Probably another one around here, so you kids watch your step."

The show over, the children scattered, riding a wave of laughter and excitement and release downstream to new adventure.

"I've never seen anything like that," Catherine said, more to herself than to Edna as they walked back toward the tables.

"Better get used to them. Lots of rattlers around, but you'll get so you can pick them out pretty easy."

"No," Catherine replied. "The snake was awful, but that little boy Joey. He wasn't playing with the other children or the snake either. It's like he was playing with . . . with . . . death."

Edna stopped, hands on hips, eyes surveying the tables, creek, women, and children that made up the ever-changing scene beneath the old cottonwood.

"Could be." And then as though she were opening an old wound, Edna continued. "Joey's mom and dad came out here just shining with hope from some central European country. Don't remember what the country was, but it sounded like they were lisping when they said it. They felt that God was holding them in the palm of His hand: first the passage to America and then the promise of free land in return for nothing but the backbreaking labor they had known all their lives.

"I used to go over and see them whenever I got to feeling sorry for myself. Their home was no better than anyone else's, but it was always filled with wildflowers and laughter. I couldn't understand much of what they said. They tried hard to speak English, but their accent was pretty bad. I loved to listen to them anyway. Watching them was like going to church—it made me feel so good.

"And when she found out she was pregnant with Joey, she ran all the way to our place. All out of breath she was and babbling away in her native tongue and laughing and too excited to sit or stand or talk without trying to do all three at once.

"I was so happy for her that I cried. I just sat there at the table and cried and cried and cried.

"I saw her a couple of weeks before Joey was born. She didn't look good even then, and when Klaus came to get me that night to help out, she looked even worse."

A tear appeared at the corner of Edna's eye and trickled down her face like a raindrop on a rock.

"Joey's mother died giving birth to him. Saddest thing I ever saw. In a way, Klaus died that night, too. He isn't finished with it yet, but he's doing his best to work himself to death so he can lie beside his Katrina.

"And Joey is alone. He couldn't be any more alone if he'd hatched from an egg. His daddy hardly ever talks to him and doesn't give him much more than what he gives his stock—something to eat and a little room to run.

"So maybe Joey does play with death. Death is about the only thing you can count on around here. Not enough rain or too much. Not enough sun or too much. But death is here, whenever you want it."

Edna pulled herself back from her reflection, struggling to make light of what she had said. "Listen to me. You must think I've lost my grip. Maybe I have."

But Catherine didn't think that. As Edna spoke, she felt herself being inundated by despair, by distance, and by loneliness and hopelessness. She felt more than ever her need to escape this terrible captivity in which she found herself.

Edna spoke again. "Men are coming down. It's time to eat."

Max and Jake Thomsen had settled with their heavily laden plates on the soft grass beside the creek. They didn't speak at first, more concerned with the chicken and potato salad and deviled eggs and radishes than with anything they might have to say.

The barn building had gone well. For all practical purposes, it was done, just some touching up with the red lead paint and hanging doors, windows, and hardware for lifting hay into the loft remained.

All this could be done after supper, or Max could do it himself if the food and beer and impromptu game of horseshoes proved to be more of an attraction than marching back through the heat to the barn.

It wasn't until their second trip through the line, after their plates had been scraped and slipped into tubs of warm water for washing, that either man felt compelled to speak.

Thomsen was first. "Well, Max, how's married life treating you?"

"I never even imagined it would be like this," Max said. "She can't keep her hands off me."

Thomsen didn't share Max's wan smile. "I noticed," he said.

"Wonder who else did?"

"Harrison. But I told him wasn't it great that you two were getting along so well, and now he doesn't know for sure what he did see."

"Thanks, Jake."

"No trouble. Anything serious?"

Max sighed. He wanted to talk. Thomsen knew that with the certainty of long experience. He had played father confessor to more people than most priests, and he could recognize the signs.

Each person was different, of course. Some would bluster into Millard's as though they hadn't a care in the world, then drink themselves into a stupor and weep their guts out on the polished mahogany bar. Others would whisper bits and pieces of their secrets into his ear each time he brought them a drink and nod knowingly when they caught his eye as though to affirm the veracity of the stories they told.

Thomsen could pick those who wanted to talk out of a bar full of people. He ignored the whiners, those who use alcohol as an excuse to pour their litany of woes into the ears of anyone who would listen, but he tried to provide a sympathetic ear to the ones who occasionally needed someone to talk to outside their tight circle of family and friends.

Max wanted to talk, but he didn't know how. Thomsen began pulling the story out of Max a little bit at a time, as gently as a mother pulls a sliver from a child's finger. And Max began to talk, the words coming slowly at first like the first drops of water over an earthen dam, and then in a torrent as the dam was torn away.

Max told Thomsen almost everything that had happened since that day of the wedding 100 years ago in Prairie Rose, but he told nothing of what had happened before, nothing of the lies that he had told, the promises he had made.

Max had always thought of himself as an honest man. He wasn't ready to admit to himself—certainly not to Thomsen—that given enough reason, he was a facile liar, and he couldn't tell Thomsen why having a wife was so important to him. Even if he had been able to put that need to words, he wouldn't be able to tell anyone about it.

So Max talked about what he had done and what Catherine had done, about the pistol and the table fork and the privy and the ranch site and about his plans. Max remembered the arguments nearly word for word. He had gone over them line after line in his mind, and the words gushed out.

Thomsen sat silently, listening to Max and nodding occasionally. Listening was Thomsen's gift. He gave freely of his ear, but was chary with his advice. Today, he made an exception.

"Maybe you ought to let her go."

Max looked at Thomsen as though he had been betrayed. "She's my wife, Jake."

"You don't own her, Max."

"She said before a priest she was mine. I can handle her. It will just take a while for her to get used to that. She'll ease up. People are just like horses. You treat them decent and let them know who's got the reins, and they come around—most of them anyway."

The words were spoken as though Max desperately wanted to believe them. They sat quietly then, Thomsen wishing he hadn't poked into the affair, Max preoccupied with something.

Max sat with his face in his hands, eyes shut. When he spoke, his voice was low, drained. "Truth be known, she scares the hell out of me. She reminds me of a filly I bought when I was on the Bar X. Maybe the prettiest animal I ever saw, but she was crazy—not locoed—just crazy. Some don't think animals can be crazy. But they can be just as crazy as people. I couldn't even put a blanket or a hackamore on her. Throw a rope on her and snub it down, and she'd fight it until her eyes bugged out and she choked.

"I tried working her every day, but she got worse instead of better. I'd go in there shaking a bucket of oats, and she'd start shaking and her eyes would roll. If I'd get close to her, she'd kick or bite. Gawd, how she could bite!

"Look at this." Max pulled his shirt out of his pants. There on his side was an ugly half-moon scar as big as an orange.

"Took hide and all. If the snubbing rope hadn't held, she'd have killed me. She sure as hell wanted to. Finally let her out to pasture. Thought she would calm down, but she didn't seem to. She'd watch me whenever I was around that pasture, watch me like I was a coyote.

"Didn't ease up at all, so I decided I might as well put her back in the corral for one more try before I sold her to some cowboy dumb as me. I loaded up a bucket of oats and headed for the pasture, shaking it so she'd hear and maybe come. She heard me all right."

Max picked up a stick and threw it hard at the creek, watching the current play with it, pulling it this way and that before it disappeared downstream.

"She was watching when I came around the corner of the barn, dancing around, kicking at something only there wasn't anything there. When she couldn't get to me, she bit herself. Never saw a horse do that before or since.

"I kept coming and finally she spooked. Went into the fence and got all tangled up. But that didn't stop her. She just kept bucking. By the time I got to her, blood was spraying from her the way water sprays when a dog shakes himself after a swim.

"She did herself proud, all right, and bucked even worse when I got close to her. Sounded like a single tree snapping when her leg broke.

"Nothing I could do for her, so I went back to the house and got a rifle. When I got back she was just standing there, on three legs, blood running from big, deep cuts.

"I walked up to her, and she didn't even move. She looked right into my eyes when I put that front sight on her forehead.

"Jake, I swear to God she was grinning at me when I pulled the trigger. I swear to God." Max shuddered. "That woman scares the hell out of me, Jake. She scares the living hell out of me."

CHAPTER 9

CATHERINE was lying alone in the dark. Outside it was midmorning, inside black as a moonless night. She had been lying there since daybreak, since awakening to the clatter of hooves and the creak of harness as Max led the giant Percherons from the corral.

She listened to the sound of Max's voice carrying across the darkness as he told the animals what great, beautiful beasts they were, and then she climbed from bed, the canvas floor covering hard and cold on her feet. She dressed, lit the kerosene lantern, and had a fire in the stove by the time Max called to her from outside.

Breakfast was quiet and peaceful, if impersonal, until Max made the mistake of thanking Catherine for not creating a scene in front of his friends.

"You thank me?" she said, bitterness spewing from a festering, self-inflicted wound. "Don't thank me—thank my sinful pride that made me whimper at the thought of admitting to those good people what a fool I am.

"Don't thank me, Mr. Bass, for being party to your deception. I am nothing more than a puppet hanging on the strings of my ugly pride."

Max took one look at Catherine's face and fled the table, leaving his food half-eaten, and Catherine, sitting in the gentle light of the kerosene lantern, her fists kneading, driving her fingernails painfully into the palms of her hands.

She fought the tears, her face still and hard, but they came anyway, trickling like a spring born of a jolt deep in the earth. Still she made no noise, sitting in silence but for the drip of tears on her plate.

When the tears stopped, Catherine rose and cleared the table, scraping dishes to wash in the water heating on the stove. It was then that she heard Max outside. She paid little attention at first, her mind recognizing, cataloging, and then ignoring the sound of saw and hammer.

But when she had finished the dishes and washed the trail of tears from her face, Catherine stepped outside to greet a pale day.

Max had carried two sawhorses and a couple armloads of lumber from the barn and was working on the creek bottom below the dugout. He stopped for a moment as Catherine emerged, and then went back to sawing one-by-four-inch boards into three-and-a-half-foot lengths, one end of each cut at a forty-five-degree angle.

At first Catherine didn't understand what he was doing, but when he began nailing the boards to some rough-cut lumber, she realized he was building a picket fence. Her face bleached white, and she marched on shaking legs down the steps from the dugout.

"You are building a corral, Mr. Bass, so you can soft-break me like a horse?"

Max was taken aback by Catherine's rage. "No, ma'am, I'm just putting up this fence. Thought it would brighten the place a little, make it seem more like home."

But Catherine didn't listen. She marched to the stump they had used to kill the chickens and pulled the double-bitted axe free, its blade still rust colored with blood.

Max had gone back to work, turning only as Catherine loomed behind him, the axe held in both hands high over her head.

"Son of a bitch!" Max screeched as he threw himself backward.

"Son of a bitch!" Catherine screamed as she swung the axe.

The blade bit deeply, and then crunched through. She swung again, and another one-by-four split.

Max was scrambling crablike backward on his haunches. Never had he felt more vulnerable.

"Now for you," she said, turning to him. Max came as close to squealing as he ever had.

"This is not a home. It is a hole in the ground. I am not married to you. That matter will be cleared up as soon as the priest comes back to Prairie Rose. Remember those two points, Mr. Bass.

"Now you git. I'll take care of these sticks. I need some kindling, anyway. Git!"

Max got.

Afterward Catherine, standing alone in the morning light, blood-stained axe in hand, felt the rage flow out of her and with it, her strength. She felt too tired to move, but she dropped the axe and forced herself up the stairs and into the dugout. She had been sitting there since in the impenetrable dark, feeling empty and helpless.

The barn raising had confirmed her worst fears. She had begged Jake Thomsen for help, and he had ignored her, avoiding her whenever chance brought them near each other.

Then Catherine had approached Edna, cautiously because she knew that Edna was Max's ally in plotting to bring her to Montana.

Would Edna mind giving her a ride to town one day?

Why didn't she wait until Max went to town? It is best not to surprise husbands so soon after marriage.

Catherine knew she was alone then in a land where distance was measured in days and four-year-old boys pick death for a playing companion.

Her nose wrinkled at the scent of raw dirt. The smell permeated her life now. Even when she left the dugout it hung on her like dust from a tomb, and that was appropriate. With the blanket drawn over the door and the lantern hanging cold and dark by the door, the dugout was as much tomb as anything, and Catherine sat in it as though she were dead. That thought comforted her. She desperately wanted to extinguish her mind as she had the lamp, to stop the mad race of thought. For a while, she succeeded, but in the end, her mind would not be muzzled. Still, she sat in silence, her body molding itself into the rough chair.

Catherine didn't hear the first drops of dirt that rained down on the step outside, her ears straining so to hear silence that she could hear nothing else. But then came a rush of clods and dust, and the blanket swayed aside, allowing a sliver of light into the room for a moment and then closing, plunging the dugout again into profound darkness.

Had it not been for her reawakened consciousness, she might not have heard the ever so faint scratching on the canvas floor.

A mouse scrambling along the top of the entrance outside had triggered a miniature landslide and had been swept down with the falling dirt, Catherine thought. Terrified by the fall, the light, and the noise, it ducked into the dugout.

Catherine was not unaccustomed to mice. She had been raised in an environment that suited mice as well as man. Still she didn't like pantries patterned with droppings and half-chewed loaves of bread, so she stamped her foot to frighten the little creature away.

But the sound of her foot was not greeted by a squeak and a scramble for the door. Instead, Catherine heard a tch, tch, tch, buzzzzz. Rattlesnake! She knew it was a rattlesnake as certainly as she knew that fires cast shadows, and she was terrified.

Somewhere between the table and the door was a rattlesnake, invisible and menacing. More scratching: The snake was moving, but where?

In a darkness that hid her own hands from her eyes, Catherine's imagination revealed the snake to her, its head drawn back in an ugly S, eyes black and impenetrable as death. In her mind's eye, Catherine watched the snake's tongue flicking, seeking the scent and warmth of her body.

It is a law of nature that cold flows to warmth, and rattlesnakes are no exception to that rule. They seek out sun-warmed rocks and the blood-warmed bodies of mice and freshly hatched birds. They are creatures without warmth or reason or compassion or hate, embodiments only of cold and darkness and death. And this rattlesnake, scratching its way across the floor of the dugout toward Catherine, was following instinct it would obey unto death.

Catherine was petrified with fear. More than anything she wanted to move, but she couldn't. Her arms pressed about her body as though they were ropes pulled by someone far more powerful than she. Her breath came in wrenching gasps torn from air as palpable as the dirt roof over her head.

Move! Move, damn you, Catherine move! Don't sit still and let that snake sink its fangs into you. Move!

More scratching. The snake was closer, but how close? Just beyond the table? Just beyond striking distance? Please, God, let it be beyond striking distance.

And then, drawing on some hidden reserve of strength, Catherine began to move, first one leg and then the other. Ever so slowly, she lifted her feet to the rung of the chair, about six inches from the floor.

Her nerves were singing. Had the snake struck, its fangs piercing Catherine's skin, her muscles would have exploded, bursting into movement.

She leaned forward on the table, bracing herself as she stood. Then she stepped up on the chair seat. From there it was a quick, easy hop to the top of the table, but her leg brushed a plate and it clattered to the floor.

The snake rattled again, more angrily this time, Catherine thought. Just under the table? No, closer to the door. Somewhere closer to the door, but not much. Somewhere close. Very, very close.

Catherine was crouched hands and knees on the table. There wasn't room for her to stand, and she wasn't sure the old table would hold her if she could. Even now it was sagging toward her bed, nails giving way under the unaccustomed weight. Catherine edged toward the more stable end, knocking a butter knife on the floor.

Buzzz!

Under the table! The damn thing was under the table. When the sagging table collapsed, the snake would be right under her, writhing and biting like that evil snake at the barn raising.

A shudder ran through Catherine.

She had to get out of the dugout, but how? And then it came to her. Her hands roamed the table, seeking anything left from breakfast that morning. Max's plate was gone, but her hand found the table knife, and she threw it skittering on the floor. The snake buzzed. The knife must have come close.

Catherine leaned down and threw the spoon. It rasped against the floor and thumped into the snake. By now the buzzing was steady, like bees around a hive on a sunny day. The snake was coiled stationary, and Catherine had the chance she had hoped for. She vaulted off the table, sprawling when the floor reached out of the darkness to slam her to the canvas. She yelped then, expecting to feel the sting of the snake's fangs, but when that didn't come, she struggled to her feet and ran to the hazy light that outlined the blanket over the entrance.

The blanket tore as she rushed through into daylight so bright it took her sight away. Blinded, she stumbled on the first step and pitched toward the bottom.

The fall took Catherine's breath away. She lay in a heap for a moment struggling to draw air into her lungs, and then she rose and began to run, stumbling at first, but smoother as her muscles reached out to meet her fear.

Down the creek bottom she ran, and across the creek, water spraying in sheets from her running feet. Her pace slowed as she climbed the hill on the other side, but then she was free, out on the level plains and away from the hole in the ground and Max and all the rest of it, and she ran and ran and ran.

The plow was slicing through the earth like a knife through living tissue. Max half expected to see blood issue from the wounds he was cutting into the prairie, to hear the earth cry out in protest, but he continued, turning the gold of this year's wheat crop into a bed for next year's seed.

The soil was dry, and Max moved in a cloud of dust that hung in the still air like a pall. It was difficult to breathe or see, and after each round Max would pull the team to a halt and climb a little way up the ridge that adjoined the field, sitting in the still, sullen heat to clear his lungs and eyes of dust and to peer at a land burned flat and bleak by the brunt of the sun.

In the distance and the harsh light, it appeared to be nothing more than the shadow of a stump etched against the prairie to the east. But Max knew it could not be a stump, the sun having washed all definition out of natural features long ago, and stumps did not move as this shadow did, painfully, slowly against the vast expanse of the land.

Max rose and took off his hat, wiping imaginary sweat from his forehead with his sleeve.

Bracing himself against the steepness of the hill, he worked his way back down to the field and walked to the team. He unhitched the horses from the plow, leaving it buried in the field like a splinter, while he drove the horses back to the corral and unharnessed them.

Then Max saddled the mare unhurriedly, working by habit while his mind plowed more fertile fields. When he climbed aboard the mare, he felt at home for the first time in days, the saddle contoured from long use to fit the swell and sway of his legs. He kicked the horse across the creek, and as she topped the hill, he felt the weight of the last few days, the anger and arguments and deceit, slip free of him.

He was on horseback, alone and easy, as he was meant to be. Max urged the mare, somnolent from the morning sun, into a lope and pointed her nose in the direction of the shadow he had seen from the ridge, and then he settled back, enjoying the wind on his face and the hunt.

Catherine had run until her breath gave out. She was walking now, hand pressing the stitch in her side, her breath coming in gasps. She was wet with sweat and muddy from the dust her shoes had kicked up along the road. She felt, more than heard, the horse as it swept by at a gallop, leaving a wake of wind as welcome as it was brief.

But it was no longer welcome when she realized it was Max who reined the mare to a stop and turned to face her.

She bolted, then, through the sagebrush and yucca and prickly pear that lined the road. Max touched his boots to the mare's flanks, and a moment later Catherine was facing the horse again. She took a few more stumbling steps, and heard the thump of the horse's hooves as the mare jumped to cut her off.

The mare was a cutting horse, and she knew the game better than Catherine, reading the direction Catherine would run by the set of her head and the tensing of her muscles. The game lasted only the few moments it took Catherine to realize that, and then she sank in a heap to the ground.

Max sat emotionless astride the mare. He felt no pleasure in running Catherine to ground and no vindictiveness. Catherine had run, and he had caught her. That was no more or less than he would have done if she had been a cow or a horse.

The silence, broken only by Catherine's labored breathing and the buzz of horseflies that came to nip the mare hung over man, woman, and horse.

Finally, and with great effort, Catherine raised her eyes to look at her captor. The sun hung over Max's shoulder and painted him sharp edged, black and implacable as a statue. She couldn't see his face and didn't know what was written on it. She knew only her exhaustion and her need.

"Ride?"

The silhouette shook its head, almost imperceptibly, and Catherine nearly burst into tears. She had put her soul into that run, and she couldn't bear the idea of the long walk back. But she rose, sagging with the weight of her desolation, and began to pick her way through the sagebrush to the road. She turned there toward the dugout, plodding along on foot while Max followed behind as though he were driving a range calf in to be cut and branded.

They reached the hill leading down to the creek just when Catherine had decided that she couldn't walk another step, that she would rather die than force one foot ahead of the other any longer. But when she saw the water, she staggered down the hill and into the creek with the fervor of a believer going to baptism. Catherine knelt on the rock bottom and scooped cool water to her face, rinsing the dirt and dust and exhaustion from it.

And Max sat silently on the mare, aloof to her ministrations, but after a moment he nudged the horse across the stream and then down to the corral. He left the mare inside, cinch loosened but still saddled, and walked back to the crossing.

Catherine had left the creek and was sitting in the swing, water dripping from her face, but as Max neared, he saw the drops were tears. Catherine was crying silently, so intently she didn't notice Max.

And at that moment, he almost burst into tears. He could not remember ever having cried, nothing having touched him that deeply before. But now he remembered that day not very long ago when Catherine had first seen the swing, how her hair flashed in patches of sunlight as she swung through the shadow of the old cottonwood. He remembered the wonder and the delight in her voice as she walked across the creek bottom and asked, "Did you make that for me?"

Her smile touched him then, dispelling briefly the dread he felt for the moment when she saw the dugout.

And when she smiled and said, "I shall ride out here every day to sit in it beside this brook," Max was so taken with her beauty he couldn't speak.

And now Catherine sat in the swing dressed in rough ranch clothes, her hair hanging in strings, and her body streaked with sweat and dust, water and mud.

The guilt Max felt as he looked at her robbed him of speech, but he continued toward her because he was drawn by her vulnerability and his need to ease her pain . . . and his own. He stood quietly, invisible until he reached out and pulled the swing to a stop.

Catherine looked up then, face white and pasty. When she spoke, her voice was lifeless. "There was a rattlesnake in the cave. He wanted to kill me. I could feel that. Why do you suppose he wanted to kill me?"

But Catherine didn't wait for an answer. She continued as though she had only a moment to tell the story.

"So I ran and ran and ran until I could run no farther, and then I walked. I felt as though the earth were crawling past me, and if I didn't walk, it would carry me back here . . . to you. And then you galloped by on your horse, and I knew that after all that running I had gone nowhere.

"I realized then that you want to kill me, too. Not like the rattlesnake. You want to corral me, make me into someone I don't want to be.

"Isn't it odd that I have spent my whole life trying to make myself into someone I'm not, and now you're trying to do the same thing to me and I struggle so against you?"

Catherine was wracked with sobs then, shudders that shook her body, and without thinking, Max stepped into the swing, his arm encircling her shoulders as he sat down. And surprised as he was at his own actions, he was even more surprised when Catherine laid her head on his shoulder and wept.

Max sat stiffly, at attention, afraid that Catherine might break if he moved, that the moment might be lost. But she wept on, running out of tears long before she ran out of grief.

When the sobs died, there was silence that grew until Max felt he could reach out and touch it, if he dared. And then Catherine spoke to Max because there was no one else to listen, and Max listened as Moses had listened on the mountain.

"Until now, I didn't think this was real. I thought you would come to your senses, and it would all be over. I would be on my way back East, and you would be plotting to bring some other woman to this godforsaken place.

"But I realize now that you don't ever intend to let me go—not in November when the priest comes, not ever."

Max tried to protest, but Catherine waved him to silence. "I would rather die than stay here. My only regret would be that I have lived so much of my life in fantasy, pretending to be someone I'm not. I would die wondering only who I am, and who I might have been."

A shudder ran through Max, and he couldn't keep the image of that crazy filly out of his mind. He could see her all tangled in barbwire, standing on three legs while blood streamed from her wounds.

And that image was in Max's voice as he whispered, "Don't talk like that."

But Catherine continued as though Max hadn't spoken. "I am alone here in the middle of this big empty. I understand now how that can drive someone like Joey to play with death."

"I'm here."

"You are my captor, and I am your prisoner. We will never be more than that to each other."

Then Catherine rose, shrugging off Max's arm as she stepped off the swing. "You've got work to do. First, get that snake out of the dugout, and then build me a door."

CHAPTER 10

FALL came without formal announcement. There was no storm to chase summer away, and trees had not yet written their leafy epitaph . . . but it was fall.

Max felt the change, seasons in Montana more sensible to feeling than to calendars. Days were wilting still in summer heat, but mornings came with an edge to them, bumping against him as he lay in his blankets on the prairie. And each evening, God painted the sky with such color that even He must weep with the joy of it.

Max had shared one of those evenings with Catherine. He had walked east with the horses that afternoon toward the dugout, watching the light play across the prairie ahead of him. Behind, the sky was practicing with subtle shades of pinks, purples, golds, and blues as an orchestra warms itself before a performance.

At the corral, Max had unharnessed the horses, giving them an extra ration of oats in celebration of having finished seeding the winter wheat. He left the gate of the corral open so they could leave to graze on the cool grass of the creek bottom, and then he hurried to the dugout, knocking before entering the door he had built a couple of weeks before.

Catherine was standing at the stove, putting the finishing touches on dinner. Max took her hand from the frying pan and placed it in his own. When she didn't resist, he led her out of the dugout, helping her up the hill that marked the boundary of the creek.

When they reached the wagon, Max lifted Catherine to the seat and then leaned against the box, his eyes fixed on the western horizon.

Serenity eases night onto the prairie. The time between light and dark is a quiet celebration of the cycle of life, creatures of the day making way for creatures of the night. Already, bats—weaving their way among the shadows, suspected more than seen—had replaced the swallows.

The sky, a tease in the afternoon, is temptress at dusk. Pale colors richen and deepen until the horizon billows with beauty. Clouds sail through golden seas, and then turn to soar into the sun, mind sketchings on a magnificent canvas.

Men who tear at the earth during the day become one with her at dusk. The beauty of God's creation pulls at their souls, as a child tugs a friend outside to play.

Catherine felt the tug and the release and the peace that comes from having seen the face of God. At the end, a shaft of light broke through the clouds and streamed to earth in benediction.

Neither Catherine nor Max moved, entranced until barking coyotes broke their reverie.

"Thank you," she said as Max helped her off the wagon. "That was the most beautiful thing I've ever seen."

"If I could," Max replied, "I would follow the sun around the earth, living always in sunsets."

Catherine looked at him quizzically, and he felt a blush spreading from his collar as the color had spread that night from the horizon.

"We best go eat," he said. "I'm hungry as a bear."

The rains came the next morning, as though by some grand plan to germinate the wheat before it was covered by winter snow. Days commenced and closed gray and wet, and the land, dry and parched from the summer sun, opened like a blotter, drinking long and deep. Springs, little more than trickles in August, grew strong again, cutting new paths through the earth, and for a time Pishkin Creek assumed the color of the land around it.

The rain continued for nearly a week, and Montana old-timers—those who had been in the state when the Indians were still wild—poked faces etched with concern from the doors of log cabins and dugouts and saloons around the prairie and shook their heads.

The gray, wet sky wasn't right, and they peered at it from the corners of their eyes, afraid to look directly at this aberration for fear of seeing something man wasn't meant to see.

Montana could be cold and hot and wet and dry from one moment to the next. But a week of rain was nothing less than a sign from God, and they lacked the cipher.

They couldn't talk about that, of course. Most of them hadn't put words to the dread the rain occasioned in them, and those who had were silent, not wanting to be thought of as *strange*.

So they huddled around dull-red stoves that normally went cold from June to mid-September and waited for a break in the weather—one way or another.

And Max and Catherine were trapped.

The land was impassable in the rain, the clay gumbo slick and sticky at the same time. Max had turned the Percherons loose after the seeding, but on the third day of the rain, they appeared above the creek, each carrying eight to ten inches of caked mud on their hooves. They walked awkwardly, slipping as they worked their way down to water.

Max put the animals into the barn and spent the better part of an hour scraping their hooves clean of the clinging mud. To ride or walk in that mud was madness. And the world pulled in on itself. Max and Catherine had only the barn, the dugout, the rain, and each other.

Before the rain, Max had been filling the loft with hay from the stack on the creek bottom. The job wasn't done, but to mix wet hay with dry was to invite trouble, and Max couldn't haul the wet heavy hay to the barn, anyway.

So he busied himself the first morning with chores, cleaning the barn and the chicken pen, but by midafternoon he had to admit that he was just wasting his time, avoiding going to the dugout while Catherine was there.

The chill of the rain seeped into Max, and finally he retreated to the dugout. The fire in the stove was welcome, but that was the only warmth in the room. Max and Catherine studiously avoided each other, speaking only when forced to by some accident of proximity.

Catherine spent the afternoon polishing the flatware as though it were silver and not the cheap metal it was. When she began to sweep the floor for the second time that afternoon, Max fled the dugout, preferring the honesty of the rain, returning only for dinner. After dinner, he rose and tucked his bedroll under his arm.

"Nice that you have a barn now," Catherine said.

"Yes, it is," Max replied, stepping through the door into the steady drizzle. Never had he seen rain like this on the prairie. It reminded him of the story of Noah, and of the petrified seashells and fish he had found in rock outcroppings. Max couldn't help wondering if the time had come for another change, that the sea that had once lain the prairie was coming back, and that he ought to be building a raft. He shook that thought away, but it came back to him several times as he stood in his wet coat, watching the rain turn the land into a stranger.

But there was relief on the second day.

Max discovered a damp spot in the dugout wall. It wasn't serious yet, but it could be. He showed the spot to Catherine and told her about the support he intended to build like a wall through the middle of the dugout.

Maybe the wall was the silver lining to the clouds that hung like a veil over the land outside. The wall would be necessary this winter when the cold drove him out of the barn and back into the dugout. He couldn't tell Catherine about his plan of course. She still harbored some hope that Max would free her when the priest came in November. It would be easier to hold her if she believed that he might let her go.

Max worked slowly and carefully, savoring the job because it kept his mind and hands partly occupied, but still he finished early. It was Catherine's turn that day to leave the dugout, to stand in the rain and contemplate her foolishness because she couldn't tolerate sitting in silence across the table from Max.

When she returned to the dugout, Max was sitting with his back to the stove. He glanced up as she stepped through the door, her hair hanging in strings and her face streaked cold and white.

"Edna says rainwater is good for washing a woman's hair," Max said.

"Are you suggesting that my hair is dirty?"

"No, ma'am. It's just that there's a lot of rainwater out there now. Most of the time there isn't."

Catherine eyed him suspiciously. "You're right. There

is precious little bounty in this country. It would be sinful not to accept what there is."

"I left some buckets out by the corral. There's probably enough by now."

"Thank you. If you would get them for me, I'll get the soap and towels ready."

Catherine heated the water on the stove, putting a wash basin, towels, and soap on the table. When the water was warm, she filled the basin and left the remainder on the stove.

Max watched her as she washed her hair—the soap sudsing more freely in the soft rainwater than in the heavily mineralized water of the creek—enjoying the intimacy of the moment as some women enjoy watching a man shave. After Catherine had rinsed her hair and wound towels around it, she sat down at the table.

"I'd like you to teach me poker," she said.

"Poker? That's not a lady's game, ma'am. Maybe we could play Old Maid or something like that."

The moment the words were out of his mouth, Max flinched. He hadn't meant anything by the reference to Old Maid, but he expected to pay for the fact, if not the intent, of his words.

Catherine's eyes narrowed, but she said only, "Poker! If you can play the game, I certainly can."

First Max laid out the rules: high card, pair, two pair, three of a kind, straight, flush, full house, straight flush, and royal flush.

Then he gave Catherine a handful of wooden matches, took a handful himself, and they began to play. The game went slowly at first, Catherine interrupting the play with questions. Max won steadily, his pile of matchsticks growing while Catherine's shrank. But Catherine was a fast learner, and once she was comfortable with the rules, Max began teaching her the finer points of the game.

"Some people play their opponents, watching for little signs that will give away a good hand or a bluff. For example, you lean up in your chair when you have a good hand and lean back when you don't.

"Trouble is that good poker players will set you up. They'll tug at their ear, and you'll bet all your chips because every time in the past that meant they were bluffing. Only this time they won't be, and you've lost your stake.

"The smart thing is to play the odds. There are only so many cards in the deck, so you can figure out what your chances are of getting the card you need, or the chances of the other guy having what he wants you to think he has.

"Now let's say that you have a four-card flush in hearts and there are three other hearts showing on the table. That means there're only six hearts left. You're playing against me, so you know what your four cards are and three of mine. That means there are forty-five cards left.

"You have six chances in forty-five or two in fifteen, or about one in eight of getting the card you need. Only makes sense to take a chance like that if the pot is at least eight times the bet, and if the flush you're betting on is likely to beat the other guy's hand.

"When you got that figured out, and your money's on the table, then you sit back to see if he leans forward or back."

Max's grin coaxed no smile from Catherine. Instead, he saw conjecture on her face. "I'm surprised at your skill in mathematics," she said.

"Never learned any mathematics, ma'am. Just poker."

The game continued until long after dark, Catherine scratching at a piece of paper beside her, and Max helping her through each hand.

But for the past half hour, Max had given Catherine her head, leaving the play completely to her. She had been losing steadily.

Now, on the table in front of her, lay two pair, queens and sevens, and she had been betting steadily as each card was shown.

Max had filled a flush with the last card.

"Up to you," he said.

Catherine leaned over the table. "I'll wager all my matchsticks against yours."

Max grinned and shoved his pile into the pot. "Gave yourself away," he said. "I knew you were bluffing when you leaned forward, just trying to make me believe you had more than what was showing."

Max reached for the pot, but Catherine shook her head. "That's what I thought you'd think."

She turned over her last card. Full house. The pot was hers.

"I'll be damned," Max said.

"Probably," Catherine said.

"Play tomorrow?"

"Why? I already have all the matches."

A perplexed expression spread across Max's face, and Catherine laughed, the sound pealing through the room like a Christmas carol played on bells.

"Might as well," she said, a smile still lighting her face. "Not much else to do in this rain."

Max was almost giddy as he walked back to the barn that night. He crawled into his blankets in the loft, warmed by the animals below, and listened to the rain drumming against the roof for a long time before drifting off to sleep. For the first time in a week, he didn't dream of the mare tangled in the barbware.

Catherine lay awake, too. She had enjoyed the game, much to her surprise, but she was thinking not of poker, but of escape.

Catherine had run from the snake on pure impulse. It wasn't until she reached the top of the hill and the prairie beyond that she had thought of her run as an attempt to escape Max and the hole in the ground and Montana.

Her mind played with the possibilities. She could seek out the priest for special dispensation. Or she could simply flee the country. Go where no one knew who she was.

She needed money and some way to reach the stage in Prairie Rose before Max caught her. . . .

The week settled into a routine built around the game.

Max would wake in the morning before daylight and rush through his chores, feeding and brushing the animals and cleaning their stalls. Then he would stand in the barn, eyes on the eastern horizon, waiting for the sun to rise like a live ember from the sea.

The earth had drunk its fill, and now the rain was splashing off its teeth and running down its face, collecting in wrinkles and creases.

Pishkin Creek was gnawing its way through the creek bottom, seeking bones hidden there centuries before. One never knew what bones would turn up when the creek ran high.

And thoughts of that and Catherine—mostly Catherine—would crowd Max's mind until the sun touched a prairie washed clean of color. Max would walk to the dugout, then, water dripping down his neck and mud sticking to his boots. His knock at the door would be greeted by Catherine's voice and the sound of sizzling sidepork.

He would slip out of his boots and slip up to the table, cradling a cup of coffee in his hands, water dripping from his face. He would sit there in silence, eyes following Catherine as she bustled about the stove, and always Catherine would feel his eyes, the heat of them bringing a deeper flush to her face.

They would eat in silence, and Max would offer to do the dishes and Catherine would refuse. When she had dried her hands, she would take her chair at the table, and Max would deal a hand of five-card stud.

They didn't talk much as they played, developing a kind of sign language over the days that made speech unnecessary. Occasionally, as one was dealing the cards, the other would pour a cup of coffee from the blue enamel pot on the stove or slip on a jacket for a hurried and wet trip to the outhouse.

And on the sixth day, Catherine pushed back from the table, a winner. "Mr. Bass, if you can win five thousand dollars playing poker, I can win ten thousand dollars."

Max laughed. "Doesn't work that way. The game's entirely different when you're playing for real money."

And then realization and hurt touched Max's eyes. "Is that why you wanted to play?"

Catherine replied in a subdued voice, "Partly."

Max sighed. "I sure as hell can't complain about your sense of honesty. You never hesitate to tell the truth."

He waited a moment to put his thoughts in order. "No, I didn't win all my money in poker, but I won most of it. Stay sober and play the odds, and you win most of the time. I win . . . most of the time."

Max rose and walked toward the door, picking his coat off the makeshift coat tree on the way. He stopped in the doorway, silhouetted by sunlight spilling into the dugout and then stepped through the door and was gone. The light outside was so bright, his eyes watered. The sun had come back in force. The heat and humidity more evocative of the tropics than Montana, and Max half expected to see dinosaurs growing from bones laid down in the mud-rock eons before. He walked up the hill, slipping in the mud, stopping at the wagon to survey this new land where the rain comes for a week at a time.

The air was incredibly clear, the rain having scrubbed the sky clean of the smoke from wildfires that flare and die in the fall. The land was darker, too, in stark contrast to the sandstone rim that defined the ridge to the north. To the west, the tilled field lay like a raw wound, but Max could almost feel the healing winter wheat growing deep within the soil.

Too bad Catherine wasn't outside to see it, but it served her right if she didn't. The horses nickered their welcome as Max opened the door to the barn.

CHAPTER 11

MAX rode at a lope, back straight, ignoring the tears the wind stole from his eyes.

The road, wet gumbo baked dry by the sun, shined hard as a china plate. But even now, if Max were to dismount and scuff hard with his boot heels, he would find rain-saturated soil an inch below the surface. Montana's thirst for water was sated for perhaps the first time in a hundred years.

The past three days had dragged. Catherine had come from the dugout tentative as a ground squirrel testing the air before leaving its burrow. Max had seen her sitting in the wagon, drinking in the sunshine through the pores of her body to warm the chill deep within her.

They hadn't argued. There were no shouts or flaring tempers. They spoke when necessary, but only then, and Max felt as though a coyote had gnawed a hole in his belly. And today, when he thought he could tolerate no more, it grew worse.

Catherine had walked in as he was rummaging through her dresser. Temper flared across her face, giving way to incredulity as he turned to face her, and she realized what he was holding.

"What are you doing with my shoes?"

"Have to go to town. I'm taking your shoes with me."

"In a pig's eye."

"The ones you're wearing, too."

"You'll have to take them from me."

"I'll do it if I have to, but that won't be pleasant for either one of us."

Catherine sighed and sat down at the table to remove her shoes. "You would enjoy that, Mr. Bass. I think you enjoy playing the bully, subjecting me to these indignities. I think you enjoy going through a woman's personal things."

Max slapped her. He hadn't meant to. He didn't even know what he was doing until it was done. He stood in disbelief, his hand stinging from the blow, watching tears spill from Catherine's eyes as she sank to the floor in a heap.

Catherine looked up at him, and the hurt he saw was more devastating than her anger had ever been.

"Mr. Bass," she said, her voice racked with sobs, "there was a time when I thought there was kindness and gentleness hidden somewhere in you. I was wrong. You have been around beasts for so long you've become one. I pity you, Mr. Bass. I pity you."

Max walked white faced from the dugout, Catherine's shoes under one arm. He saddled the mare, dropped the shoes into the saddlebags, and kicked the horse into a lope toward town. He felt nothing, not the easy gait of the horse, not the wind in his face, not the tears on his cheeks—nothing.

It was dark when he reached town, and he rode down Main Street, looking neither right nor left until he reached Millard's. Max tied the mare to a post and loosened the cinch on the saddle, thumping across the boardwalk and past the double doors, both ajar to invite the cool night air inside.

It was a busy night, the bar lined with men and two or three of the tables filled. They all looked up as Max stepped through the door, their attention lingering longer than he thought it should. He walked to an open stool, and just before he sat down, Len Hawks yelled, "What's the matter, Max, you look tired!"

Hawks hooted and there was scattered laughter at his table, but the line of men at the bar appeared uncomfortable, trying hard to pretend they hadn't heard.

Thomsen appeared and leaned down, both massive arms braced on the bar. "What'll you have, Max?"

"Glass of beer," Max said, and then quietly so only Thomsen could hear him, Max asked, "What's up?" inclining his head toward the table.

But Thomsen didn't answer, turning instead to draw Max's beer. Before he returned, the banker Phillips walked through the back door of the bar, returning from the outhouse behind the building.

Max refused to do business with Phillips, trusting most bankers very little and Phillips not at all. Since the banker had arrived in Prairie Rose, he had been involved in some shady, if not downright dishonest, deals.

Phillips spotted Max and strutted over. "Howdy, Max," he said, hand on Max's shoulder. Max stiffened. He didn't like to be touched, least of all by Phillips.

"Suppose you got your wheat in before the rain?"

Max nodded.

Phillips grinned and said in a stage whisper, "Can't beat experience, can you, Max?" Hawks hooted again, and Phillips joined that table.

Thomsen returned just as Max was beginning to step off the stool. He grabbed Max's arm. "Give me a hand out back?"

Max nodded. There wasn't anything in the back room, or Prairie Rose for that matter, that Thomsen couldn't handle by himself. He wanted to talk.

The back room was filled with boxes of whiskey and oiled sawdust for sweeping the floor and a cot Thomsen threw drunks on to sleep off their night on the town. The room was lit by a kerosene lamp hanging from the ceiling. Thomsen had bumped it with his head, and it was swinging, leaving the room distorted and oblique. Max felt himself swaying with the light. He was glad he hadn't had anything to drink.

"What is it?" Max asked.

"Phillips has been in here all night," Thomsen said, hesitating before continuing. "He's been saying that an . . . uh . . . inexperienced girl wouldn't have come all the way out here from Boston to marry you. He's been saying that Catherine is *very* experienced."

Max's face went white, and a shudder shook his body. His eyes glazed and the muscles at the hinge of his jaw knotted. He turned to go back into the bar.

"No!" Jake grabbed his arm, and Max tugged to get free. They struggled for a moment, and then Max cocked his fist.

"Max! It's me!" Thomsen hissed. "Don't do that. Just give me a minute."

Max shook his head. His fury had disconnected the link between mind and body. Thomsen was desperately trying to bring reason back.

"Max, you do that, and every man jack in here will think Phillips is telling the truth."

Max's fist knotted again.

"Max! Think! You know Phillips is lying, and I know, but they don't. If you jump out there to defend your wife's honor, word will get around that it *needed* defending. I'd like to feel Phillips's fat little neck under my hands, but . . ."

"I'll take his neck!"

"Max, if you give a damn about Catherine, you better listen. You bull in there and put your boots to the banker, and Catherine will be the one with the bruises. Think about her for a change."

Max's voice squeezed between clenched teeth. "What the hell do you think I've been thinking of? I haven't thought of anything else since she stepped off the stage.

"Jake, she's a good woman, and the idea that that bloated banker is playing fast and loose with her reputation makes me want to break him apart, a little at a time."

Rage overtook Max again. He growled and jerked to free his arm from Thomsen's grip.

"Max, there's a better way. We can shake Catherine loose and let the banker punch himself in the nose. The first thing is that you've got to put on your best poker face, and then we'll need a little help from my friend K.O. here."

Thomsen held up a small glass vial filled with a clear liquid.

They stepped out of the back room ten minutes later. Phillips watched as Max took his seat at the bar. He started to rise. "Best be going. It's past my bedtime."

But Thomsen overheard the banker. "Thanks, Aloysius. I was going to buy a round for the table, but if you're going, I'll save a little money."

"He ain't going anywhere," Hawks said, jerking Phillips back into his chair. "Long as you're buying, the night's young."

Thomsen shrugged. Max sat at the bar, playing poker in his mind. Jake had dealt him a winning hand. All he had to do was keep a poker face and a low profile, at least for the next half hour. He was halfway into his second beer when Hawks called from the table again.

"Max, your ears are red. Must have been hot in that back room, or maybe somebody is talking about you."

Max turned around on his stool and lifted his mug to toast the table. The grin on his face was hard as the rimrock above the dugout.

"Ears get red, I know I've had enough to drink." He pulled a double eagle out of his pocket and tossed it to Thomsen. "Give me a bottle, and let 'em drink up the change."

Thomsen growled loud enough for everyone in the saloon to hear, "When Max Bass buys for the house, you *know* he's had too much to drink."

A spattering of good-natured laughter followed Max into the darkness. Everything was going according to plan. Now, to hide the horse in the copse of trees down by the river and sneak into the back room to await the results of the drops that Thomsen had just put in the banker's drink.

It was nearly two o'clock in the morning when Max pointed the mare's nose home. Above, the sky was lit with stars and wide as forever. Below walked Max and the mare, their journey not even a scratch on time.

As they plodded along, Max drank at the bottle, sips at first and then long pulls. He paused at the hill above the solitary cottonwood. Catherine was awakened by the sound of his laughter, echoing up the creek bottom loud enough to quiet the coyote that had been barking from the ridge.

"Son of a bitch," the banker Phillips whispered.

The cold had awakened him, and he quickly realized

he had the granddaddy of all hangovers. He lay with his eyes shut tight against the pain. He would have liked to have groaned, but he didn't think he could tolerate the noise.

"Son of a bitch," the banker Phillips whispered again.

As his head began to clear, he realized that he was cold. What the hell? Somebody had stolen his covers. His eyes opened in slits. Middle of the night; the stars were still bright.

Stars?

Phillips lurched into a sitting position, and the movement transformed his head into a bass drum. The banker tried to ignore his hangover long enough to take stock. He wasn't in his bed: He was alone out on the prairie, and . . . he was naked! Stark naked! Not a stitch! Not even socks! As that realization jolted into his brain, Phillips reached down reflexively to cover himself and lost his balance. He rolled over a prickly pear.

"Son of a bitch!" the banker Phillips roared. He felt his head split and his brain fall out, bouncing on the ground: BOOM! BOOM! When the spasm passed and some semblance of reason had returned, the banker eased himself to his feet, carrying his head as though it were chock full of dynamite and would explode at the slightest jolt.

Nothing. Not a road, not a tree, not a hill, nothing. Phillips was in the middle of the big empty, and he didn't know how he had gotten there or how he would get out. He wrapped his arms around himself. He didn't want to shiver. If he started shaking, his aching head would fall off.

He'd had hangovers before, but never anything like this, not even when he drank that green grain alcohol brewed on the Musselshell and seasoned with juniper berries. A wave of nausea swept over him, and he crouched hands on knees until it passed.

He had blacked out before, but never had he awakened on the prairie in the middle of the night stark naked.

Fear was building in Phillips, rising from his gut and winding around his throat. The prairie was home to wolves and coyotes and cougars and rattlesnakes and cactus and yucca, sharp pointed fangs and claws and spines. Late as it was, he could even be caught in one of those early fall blizzards.

Phillips didn't like the prairie under the best of conditions. Tonight, he hated it.

The sound played in his ears until his fears quieted enough for him to hear it. Strange sound, like the Klaxons on some of those motorcars he had seen in Billings.

Geese! Something in the night had disturbed geese. Must be the Lanning place, only place Phillips knew of that raised geese.

The banker's hopes soared. He could walk over to the Lanning place and ask for a ride to town. Getting out of this mess would be as simple as . . . whoops! Couldn't do that. Couldn't have a story spreading around town about a banker who gets drunk and winds up naked and lost on the prairie.

Phillips would have to get out of this himself. He took a deep breath of cold night air. Had to get his brain functioning. The Lanning place was south of town. He was facing the sound of the geese and the North Star hung over his left shoulder. All he had to do was go straight ahead until he reached the road and then turn north toward town. He had to hurry though. The Lanning place was a good four miles from town, and that would make it close to dawn by the time he reached Prairie Rose.

His course set, the banker reminded himself that the longest journey begins with the first step. His first landed his foot on a sharp rock. He roared, hopping on his good foot until he lost his balance and pitched headfirst into a patch of greasewood. The thorns scratched furrows down his back wide enough for plowing.

There was some good that came of it. His high, inhuman screech set the geese honking again.

The banker crawled gingerly out of the greasewood. Too dangerous to wait here and too dangerous to walk. Nothing left to do but crawl. Phillips dropped to all fours, his free hand ranging warily in front of him, muttered curses marking its encounters with prickly pears.

And so he made his way toward the road, white hide shining dully in the starlight, unfettered belly sagging, grunts and snorts enhancing the illusion that something primitive and porcine was loose on the Montana prairie.

Phillips reached the road forty-five minutes later. Gratefully, he stood. His back, unaccustomed to crawling, had been protesting for the past twenty minutes, so he couldn't stand straight. Still, even walking hunched over, shuffling along the road was better than crawling across the prairie. So on he walked, groaning with the ache of his back and muttering each time his foot found a rock in the road. When he heard the high-pitched Eeeee-eeee from the side of the road, he assumed it was the call of some night bird. Phillips looked at the stars and picked up his pace. Dawn was not long in coming, and he was still four miles from town.

Matilda Harris had arisen early that morning. She always did after one of "those nights." She had seen it coming. Edwin had been particularly attentive, fetching her a second cup of coffee after dinner and offering to dry the dishes. Not that she would let him, of course. The kitchen was hers, and she didn't like anyone else bumping around in it. She had tried putting it off, sitting downstairs in the parlor reading the Bible. She thought if Edwin saw her with the good book it might set his mind on more spiritual matters, but it didn't.

About midnight, he came downstairs, took the Bible away from her, and led her to bed where he had his way with her, grunting and groaning until he got done whatever he felt so compelled to do. She always lay in bed those times, eyes shut, thinking about the week's menus. Run a boardinghouse and the work was never done, not for the woman anyway.

When he was done and had rolled over and gone to sleep, she slept for a while, but was up at two o'clock. No sense lying in bed if you couldn't sleep and there was work to do. She was downstairs doing laundry. Took her two days to do laundry, personal things first, already out back hanging on the line, and then the linen from the boardinghouse.

Mrs. Harris yawned: looked like it was going to be a long day.

"Son of a bitch," whispered the banker Phillips.

The last four miles had taken close to two hours on feet as raw as hamburger. And now the birds were singing, and the stars were dull, disappearing. False dawn was only moments away. Chances were that his clothes were in Millard's. He could get dressed there and walk back to the boardinghouse. If anyone saw him entering the boardinghouse, he could say he was out for a morning constitutional. No slugabed he, he would tell them, and they would tell the rest of the town that there were no banking hours for the banker Phillips. A smile crossed his face. Leave it to him to turn a problem into an asset.

If his clothes weren't there, he could slip down the alley between Millard's and the boardinghouse. Not much chance that townsfolk would be out and about at that time. But Phillips was a cautious man. (He never talked face-to-face about a man or woman if he could talk behind their backs. He never lent money to anybody who really needed it, and he always covered his tracks.) It was perfectly natural for him to play it safe. He stopped by the side of the road and picked two sprays of sagebrush. Fanning them fore and aft, he slipped into town, bound for Millard's.

The gray light of false dawn covered the land as Phillips reached the saloon. He slipped around to the back door.

Locked! The damn thing was locked. Phillips pounded on the door, trying to strike the balance between being loud enough to be heard by Thomsen inside, and not so loud as to be heard by anyone down the street. Too loud. A dog was barking up the street. Thank heaven, he was too far away to be any immediate problem.

Phillips covered himself with the sagebrush. "Thomsen, open up!" Nothing. Phillips pressed his ear to the door. He thought he could hear a muffled whoofing inside. Must be Thomsen snoring.

No other solution, he must slip back to the boardinghouse and get into his room before anyone else awoke.

Phillips was deep in thought. He had always been

proud of his ability to shut himself away from what was going on around him, to concentrate so fully on the matter at hand that nothing could distract him.

He was pure concentration as he walked down the alley, sagebrush fan front and rear, considering the cause of the bizarre events of that night. Thomsen must have slipped him knockout drops. Bass probably hauled him out of town. He vaguely remembered the rocking gait of a horse and the thump when he hit the ground.

Thomsen and Bass would pay for this night. They would rue the day they moved the president of the Prairie Rose Bank to vengeance.

Matilda Harris was taking her underthings off the clothesline behind the boardinghouse. No reason to leave them on the line where everyone could see them. She was a woman from a good family, not like the widow Mrs. Lecker across the alley. She didn't seem to care who saw her wash. Wanton, she was.

Mrs. Harris didn't notice the banker Phillips until he popped through the bushes that lined the alley, and then she saw more of him than she ever wanted to.

"Mr. Phillips," she gasped.

Phillips was so caught up in his plans for revenge, he forgot himself. He reached up to tip his hat.

Mrs. Harris's scream rattled windows for two blocks around. It brought Mr. Harris out of bed with a thump. It jarred the banker, who hastily covered himself as best he could.

Harris burst through the door of the couple's apartment. "Hang on, Tillie, I'm coming!"

Mrs. Harris fell in a swoon by the clothesline, and the banker tossed his sagebrush apparel aside and scooted for the back stairs. Mrs. Lecker saw him and waved from across the alley.

Inside, Phillips careened down the hall. He could lock himself in his room and get dressed. By then he would have some kind of explanation.

But when he skidded to a stop at his door and reached for his key, he realized he didn't have any pockets.

"Son of a bitch," whispered the banker Phillips.

"Phillips!" roared Edwin Harris, charging up the stairs. "Flaunt yourself at my wife, will you . . . you . . . bastard!"

CHAPTER 12

MAX was ambling into consciousness, prodded along by a stalk of hay poking him between his shoulder blades.

As his senses tuned in for the day, his nose caught a scent that seasoned and then overcame the redolence of the hay. Strong it was, from the cork of a half-full whiskey bottle lying beside him. Max's stomach shuddered, and he nearly vomited. He couldn't tolerate whiskey—never had been able to. But when he left Millard's the night before, buying a bottle seemed to be the thing to do, and as long as he had it, Max felt compelled to drink it. He was not a wasteful man.

But he was paying for his frugality this morning. Another spasm, and Max rolled over and drew himself up to his hands and knees, just in case.

Be a shame to vomit in the hay, so he donned his hat and pulled on his boots. He teetered a bit as he walked over to the ladder leading down from the loft. He started down, swaying when the odor of fresh horse dung caught him full in the face, but he continued down.

The walk to the creek was tentative, Max carrying the bottle by the neck as though it were a snake. He knelt on the edge of the creek, thrust the bottle beneath the surface of the water and pulled the cork. He waited until creek water replaced the whiskey in the bottle and then emptied it, consigning it to the current. The bottle bobbed along. Max wondered how far it would go before lodging against a bank or against a rock, and how long before some cowpoke found it and wondered what kind of a Saturday night had been hidden inside.

Max shed his shirt, shivering as much from the thought of the cold water as from the cool morning air, then stuck his head neck deep into the water.

Max came up sucking air, water coursing over his chest and back, raising gooseflesh. But his eyes were clear, and his mind ready for what lay ahead at the dugout.

Smoke was coming from the chimney. Catherine was awake. Might as well get it over with.

Max's knock at the door was met with silence. He knocked again, and then poked his head through. Catherine was standing at the stove, sprinkling salt and pepper on sidepork sizzling in a pan. She didn't bother to look up.

Max took his place at the table. Only one plate and setting. A moment later, Catherine carried the pan to the table and shoveled the sidepork and some fried potatoes onto her plate. She sat down then and began eating.

"Nice morning."

Catherine didn't look up.

"Guess I'll fix me some breakfast."

Catherine continued eating as though she were sitting alone at the table. Max carried the pan back to the stove, but found only a few remaining potato scraps. He ate those with his fingers. He returned to the table just as Catherine was rising. "Wasn't very hungry, anyway."

Catherine walked back to the water warming on the stove, and washed her plate and the two frying pans, drying them with the heat from the stove.

"Thought we might go over to the Leningtons today. Something there I'd like to show you."

Catherine was slipping on her jacket, and she stepped barefoot out the door on her way to the outhouse, anywhere Max wasn't.

Shoes! Max had forgotten to bring Catherine her shoes. No wonder she was angry. He trotted over to the barn and pulled the shoes from his saddlebags and then hesitated, deciding to hitch up the mare as long as he was already in the barn. Max dawdled at the job for forty-five minutes, about forty more than usual, and when he could stall no longer, he walked back.

Catherine was sitting at the table, sipping a cup of coffee when Max stepped through the door. He walked tentatively to the table. She didn't look up. Max pulled his chair back to the table and sat down, chin resting on the top of the chair's back.

"I'm terrible sorry. I didn't mean to slap you. I've never slapped any woman, and if I ever wanted to slap one, you would be the last on the list."

Max ran his fingers through his hair, muttering something even he couldn't hear. "This isn't coming out right. What I mean to say is that I didn't mean to do it, and I feel lower than a snake's belly. I took the shoes because I had to go to town, and I couldn't have you running away. But I meant to give them back as soon as I could."

Max laid both pairs on the table.

Catherine picked them up with one hand, leaned across to the stove and tossed them in. Max's eyes widened in disbelief, and he sat transfixed, unable to move until the smell of burning leather tipped him off his chair. Max leaped toward the stove, his chair toppling and skidding across the floor. He opened the firebox and peeked in as though he were peering into the depths of hell. The shoes had curled in the heat, and then as the fresh air fanned the fire, they burst into flame.

"Those are the only shoes you have," Max said.

Catherine rose, slipped on her jacket and stepped out into a blustery fall day. When Max followed a few minutes later, she was already sitting on the seat of the wagon, bare feet clear of the skirt billowing in the wind.

"I've got a pair of dress boots. They wouldn't fit, but you could wear them until we can get something for you."

Silence. Silence followed by silence. Max sighed, climbed aboard, and picked up the reins.

If he had been alone, Max would have gone cross country. The trip was rough, but passable. But with Catherine aboard, he chose the road and on they drove, pelted with swirling dust each time a gust of wind passed. There was winter in the air, but more nibble than bite. Still, Catherine's feet, exposed to the wind, grew stiff and cold. The chill was spreading through her as they approached the Leningtons, and she felt metallically stiff as she climbed off the wagon.

The Lenington place was typical: a three-room, tar-paper shack belching coal smoke, a lean-to open ended and pointing south into a corral, and a root cellar.

Edna was bent over a shovel in the garden, and didn't look up until little Zeb sprinted over to her with the news. She pushed herself upright with the handle of the shovel and waved, a bit tentatively because of the hitch in her back. Spading the garden always left her stiff and sore, and the pain grew a little worse each year. She walked over to the wagon, dreading each step, trying to show the warmth she felt for Max and his bride and not the pain in her back.

"Isn't this something," she said, steadying herself against the wagon box. "Two sets of visitors in one day. Just like we were living in town. Come on in and have some coffee. Zeb's abed, but I'd wager he'll pop out when he sees you two."

Zeb spent a lot of time in bed, particularly when there was a garden to be spaded or a field to be plowed or anything else that might fall to him. He was fortunate that the older boys could do nearly a man's work, but a neighbor had hired them for the past three days to haul coal, and Edna was too stubborn just to forget about the garden until they came back. Zeb didn't like to think of himself as lazy, it was just that he didn't like to work very much, and he had always considered himself a little too sensitive for heavy toil. Given his druthers, he'd rather spend the day puttering around the house.

He was sitting at the table in his long johns playing solitaire when Edna led her visitors through the door. He scooted toward his room like a rabbit running for his life.

"Zeb's pretty spry for an old man ailing so," Edna said with a wink. She had long since forgiven him his lack of industry. He was, as she had once told Max, about as useful as teats on a boar, but he only drank when he had the opportunity, and he had never said a bad word about another human being as far as she knew.

Max smiled. "We'll be needing another hog soon as the weather breaks, maybe two."

"That'll bring him out," Edna said.

Zeb was a master meat processor. The Leningtons had the only decent-sized herd of hogs in the area, and

Zeb was the best bacon and ham maker for perhaps a thousand miles. He had learned his trade in the hills of Tennessee, and he trusted no one else to turn the porkers into honey-cured ham.

And then, as though to emphasize Edna's thought, Zeb stepped into the kitchen, tucking his shirttail into his pants. His face had some color to it, and Max figured that was as close to a blush as Zeb would ever come.

"Caught me unawares," he said, pulling up a chair at the table that ranged from one end of the room almost to the other.

"Second time today," Edna said. "Charley Lucas was over this morning and caught Zeb in his long handles, too. Won't be long before people start calling you banker Phillips."

"Banker Phillips?" Catherine asked.

"Oh, good," Edna said, beaming. "I was afraid you might have already heard about it. Let me pour the coffee, and I'll tell you all about it."

She came back with the coffeepot in one hand and four cups in the other. It wasn't often that she had a story as good as this one, and she went over it in her mind as she poured the coffee.

Most gossip on the prairie was pretty tame. Living so far apart, it wasn't often that outsiders were privy to a family's secrets. So most of the news was exaggerated, overplayed to make it more exciting.

But Edna knew she was in possession of a classic, the stuff of which stories would be told for years. She wanted to play it for full dramatic effect, but she didn't want to exaggerate it to detract from the credibility of the story.

When she put the coffeepot down on the table, she had the tale plotted like a good novel.

"There was something strange in the air last night," she said, peering around the table to make sure she had everyone's attention. "I felt it when I went outside to . . . to make my last trip before I went to bed.

"The air was kind of still and expectant, as though something were afoot, something different. It was riding heavy on me until all the kids were inside and tucked in, and even then I felt uneasy somehow.

"I didn't think about that anymore until Charley Lucas came in this morning, spreading the news like he was Paul Revere. It wasn't until then I realized how right I'd been."

Edna paused and took a long sip of coffee, letting the silence stretch the suspense, and then she continued, "There are two stories. Some people say they're connected, and maybe they are. Seems that long about two o'clock this morning, the Lannings' geese tuned up. They're better than a watchdog, you know, for guarding a place and a lot better to eat."

Edna's joke went unnoticed. She continued, but it was clear she was a little miffed. "They've been having some trouble with a coyote or a neighbor dog out there, so Mrs. Lanning got up to see what it was. Ol' Henry would sleep through a thunderstorm, probably couldn't hear it anyway over his snoring. I swear when he goes to sleep Sunday morning in church, the rest of us might as well leave—can't hear the preacher or the choir either over the racket.

"Anyway, when Mrs. Lanning stepped outside, the geese were all stretching their necks and honking at something out by the road, so she grabbed a stick and started out quiet as she could. She hadn't gone but a few steps when she heard this inhuman shriek, like something tormented.

"Remember, I told you how funny it was last night, like there was something on the prairie that shouldn't be? Well, Mrs. Lanning felt that, too, even before she heard the shriek, and the closer she came to the road, the stronger the feeling got to be. It was real spooky out there, nothing but the sound of the geese behind her and a little wind stirring the sagebrush."

Edna wished it were dark: This story would best be told in the dark. But you can't always have things the way you'd like, so she took a deep breath and continued.

"It was then she heard it, coming through the brush on the other side of the road. Grunting and wheezing it was, and Mrs. Lanning thought it must be a pig, but she didn't know anybody in this country besides us that might have a full-grown hog.

"And then she saw it. White it was and huge, moving across the prairie, rocking back and forth and squealing every so often like it was being tormented by the devil.

"I imagine her eyes were big as dinner plates. Well, this creature gets to the road, and . . ."

Edna stopped to stare directly into Catherine's eyes. "Then this creature stands up and walks down the road like it was a man—or something not quite a man. It was bent over, she said, arms kind of swinging at its sides. She figured it was at least eight feet tall. It walks down the road growling to itself, almost like it was trying to talk.

"Mrs. Lanning let out a shriek, and it just kept walking, not even looking back at her, and she lit out for the house. She figured she'd get the shotgun in case it came after her.

"Stayed awake all night, she did. Sitting at a chair in the kitchen, loaded shotgun on the table, not knowing if she was going to live or die, and ol' Henry slept through the whole thing."

There was silence at the table, each deep in thought over the pictures Edna had conjured. It was Catherine who broke the silence.

"Banshee," she said, almost in a whisper.

Max's skin crawled. Catherine's face was white, and her eyes big and round.

"What do you mean, child?" Edna whispered.

"Banshee, it was," Catherine said. "The shriek she heard was a banshee, calling the soul of someone about to die."

"Did anyone die at the Lannings?"

Edna shook her head.

"Then the banshee must have been summoning that creature to walk this land last night—for what purpose, we can only guess."

Edna felt the hair go up on the back of her neck. She had intended to play up the bizarre aspects of the story, but she hadn't counted on this. Catherine obviously believed in banshees, and now Edna wasn't sure that she didn't. Nobody knew what it was that had waddled grunting across the prairie.

Max cut in, "Maybe we better go look at the horses. I think we'll take them home today."

Edna nodded. She would tell them the rest of the story when they came back. Wasn't a good time now, anyway.

"Walk out with you," Zeb said. "You can pick out your hogs while you're here, and then I can butcher soon as it cools off. I'll get the children out after some chokecherry."

It seemed too light outside, paradoxical to step into sunlight after speaking of creatures of the dark. Still, the sun didn't chase away the chill Max felt, the chill that settled on him when he looked over the table and into Catherine's eyes.

They walked to the corral, Catherine stepping carefully over and around a general collection of manure that peppered the yard. As they approached the corral, the horses trotted toward them, poking their noses over the top rail to be petted. They were beautiful creatures with long, aristocratic noses and long, strong legs. They were even more beautiful than the blooded horse the young man in Ireland had been sitting. Catherine reached tentatively toward the smaller of the animals, and the mare reached out to check the hand for a cookie or sugar.

"More pets than anything," Zeb said.

"No," Max said. "They're more horse than most people will see in a lifetime. They've never felt a spur or a whip, but these two would run their lives out for nothing more than the touch of a heel."

His face glowed as he warmed to his subject. "They are fast, not as fast as thoroughbreds running on a track, maybe, but they'll outrun most anything on this prairie.

"And their gait is so easy, you'd swear you're riding a cloud. They look like clouds, too. Gray as rainstorms in summer and as filled with promise."

He stopped, took off his hat, and wiped imaginary sweat off his forehead with his sleeve.

"The mare is yours," he said, looking at Catherine, "no matter what."

Catherine stepped forward and hugged the mare's neck, and the horse reached down to check her pockets for a treat.

When Catherine looked at Max, there were tears in her eyes. "Thank you," she said. "What is she called?"

"Didn't name them. You can if you like."

"I'll call her Lady," Catherine said, "and him, Gentleman's Promise."

"She's with foal," Max said. "The colt will be as close to magic as a horse can get."

"How do you know it'll be a colt?" Zeb asked with a grin.

"Because these two horses don't ever do anything wrong. They'll give me a stud that people will come miles to see, just to know what a horse really should be like."

And then Max and Zeb laughed, the sound of it breaking through the soft wail of the wind on the land.

"May I ride her?" Catherine asked.

"Know how?"

Catherine shook her head.

"No matter. She'll teach you. I'm not sure I ever knew what riding was until I bought these two."

Max climbed into the corral and walked to the stud. The horse leaned forward to allow Max to pay homage, and he snugged a loop behind Promise's head, running the rope down along the jaw and tying a half hitch around the stud's nose. Then, holding the line and a handful of mane in his left hand, he vaulted astride the horse.

Max and the stud seemed to be more one creature than two, and that image was enhanced as he guided the animal to the corral gate with his heels and knees. Without dismounting, Max unlatched the gate and nudged the horse through. The mare nickered, and Max left the gate open for her.

The animals danced about the yard, two prima ballerinas celebrating beauty and movement and life on a barnyard stage. And Max directed the performance without intruding on it. And then he gave the horses their heads and touched his heels to the stud's flanks. They flew from the yard in sheer celebration of life, running easy on the earth, in harmony with her, sweeping over the land until they neared the section line where Max set them on a wide curve back toward the Leningtons'. Neck and neck, they pulled into the yard, resenting the return to earth, dancing with the joy of the run.

"They *are* magic," Catherine whispered.

"Yes," Max said with a quiet intensity, studying Catherine's face. "They are."

Edna's voice cut into the moment.

"Coffee's poured. It's time for the rest of the story."

"Better go," Zeb said. "That woman would be terrible disappointed if she couldn't tell you the latest."

Zeb followed Max and Catherine back to the house, a tiny smile tugging at the corners of his mouth.

Edna was already sitting at the table, surrounded by steaming cups and empty chairs. There was a sense of excitement in Max and Catherine, and that was good. Catherine's banshee had been exorcised by the magic of the Appaloosas.

"Saved the best part for the last," Edna said, pulling their attention to her. "It seems that the banker Phillips went prowling last night. . . ."

Edna told them every detail, sketching in a bit of the background when necessary to season the story.

"Well, you know what Mrs. Harris is like. She faints when a bitch comes into heat. Zeb says that if she'd been Eve, there'd be nothing left of the human race but some of those petrified bones we find around here."

Lenington nodded. That's what he said, all right.

"When Phillips tipped his hat, Mrs. Harris shrieked to high heaven and just kind of melted down into a little heap by the clothesline. The banker headed up those back stairs like he was running on the coals of hell.

"Wasn't but a second later that Harris busted through the back door, hell bent to save his Tillie just as the back door slammed shut behind the banker. Harris went up those steps three at a time, and ran right up to the banker, who was standing there stark naked.

"You got to hand it to the banker though. He talked Harris to a standstill. Harris went up those stairs ready to do mayhem, and the banker talked him out of it—at least for a while.

"Edwin, he's pretty husky and strong as a bull, but he isn't particularly bright. And that banker is a smooth talker. He talks out of both sides of his mouth so fast you'd swear you were talking to two people. He had the most outlandish story I've ever heard . . . and Max, it concerns you."

Max didn't need to feign surprise. What had led the banker to suspect him?

Edna had been watching Max as she spoke. His surprise had been genuine. The banker was lying.

"Phillips said he was the victim of some hoax and that Max and Thomsen were responsible. Wild story, it was, about the banker being slipped some knockout drops, and then hauled unconscious and naked out of town. Said he could prove it."

Max leaned back in his chair and crossed his legs. People who had played poker with him for any length of time would have reached for a stack of chips. Max Bass was getting ready to bluff.

"Phillips said he had his clothes on," Edna continued,

"when Thomsen slipped him the mickey. He said his clothes were still at Thomsen's. He wasn't some kind of pervert he said, to take off his clothes and go prowling. 'Check Millard's,' the banker said."

That raised the hair on the back of Max's neck. "But that doesn't prove anything. . . ."

Edna cut him short. "I know that, and you know that, but Harris didn't catch on. Harris carries the key to the rooms on a leather thong around his neck. So he lets the banker into his room to get dressed, and there on the bed, neat as you please," Edna paused a moment, "were the banker's clothes."

Max uncrossed his legs and leaned forward. Thomsen hadn't told him about the clothes.

"When Phillips saw those clothes, he squealed like a stuck pig. And you can imagine what Harris did."

They all nodded. They could, indeed, imagine what Harris did.

"Seems that the banker Phillips had been spreading stories about . . . certain people," Edna said, her eyes focused on Max. "Nobody believes those stories anymore. A man who flaunts himself in front of ladies doesn't have much credibility."

Max's face was a mask, Catherine's a question.

And then Edna turned to Catherine. "I've been talking all afternoon, and I haven't given you two a chance to say anything. Would you please, child, tell me why you aren't wearing shoes?"

Catherine caught Max's eyes. She had intended to tell Edna about his taking her shoes. The story would have spread through eastern Montana, and Max's reputation would have been ruined, among women at any rate. But this afternoon, Max had promised her Lady, and she had been moved by that and the way he melded with the horses. He had been part of the magic, too.

"It's a bet," Catherine said. "Max bet me five dollars and two pairs of new shoes that nobody would notice if I went barefoot."

"Strange bet," Edna said.

"Well, you know Max," Catherine said. Then she turned to him. "Cross my palm with silver, Mr. Bass."

Max fidgeted. He hated to part with that much cash money at one time unless he received good value for it. But after he had considered the point for a moment, he realized his reputation was worth five dollars, although he would have preferred paying less.

Catherine grinned and accepted the money. "I will pick out the shoes next time we go to town."

Max nodded, but he wasn't pleased about it.

Good-byes said, and the Appaloosas tied behind the wagon, Max and Catherine set out on the high prairie for the dugout. About halfway there, Max pulled the mare to a stop.

Max, Catherine, the horses, and the wagon were the only signs of civilization for as far as the eye could reach. They were alone in the big empty, and in that intimacy and anonymity, Max forced himself to speak.

"That wasn't a banshee at the Lannings last night," he said, eyes fixed on the horizon. "That's where I dumped the banker Phillips, naked, after Jake slipped him the knockout drops."

"But why?"

Max hesitated. He had meant to spare her, but he wanted her to understand, and he didn't want her to speak anymore of banshees.

Catherine broke in, “It was I he was spreading stories about, wasn't it?”

Max looked at her in surprise.

“I thought so,” she said. Then she told Max about the stagecoach ride into Prairie Rose and how Phillips had gloried in humiliating her and how she had retaliated by sticking her hat pin deep into his leg. As a grin spread across Max's face, Catherine told him about the incident in the bank.

“You stuck him with a hat pin?”

Catherine nodded, and Max laughed, peals of unrestrained laughter. Then Catherine laughed until the prairie filled with it. They rode to the dugout like that, the laughter of one pulling the other along.

CHAPTER 13

MAX was up before daylight, eager to be with his horses. He shook the hay from his clothing before slipping on his shirt and pants, shivering a bit as shirt touched skin still warm from the bed. There was a bite to the air, and it followed him down the ladder and into the barn proper. Wouldn't be long before he had to change his sleeping arrangements. That was one battle he wasn't eager to join.

He filled two buckets with oats and shook them as he walked toward the corral. The mare nickered and danced over to him, a prima ballerina and adoring aficionado. He dumped the oats into a feed trough and told the horses how beautiful they were until the sun cracked the eastern horizon. Then he pitched hay into the corral with a fork left standing by the stack. He was occupied with that as Catherine walked up the path to the outhouse. She joined him at the corral a moment later.

"Winter has passed already, Mr. Bass?"

Max had been so bewitched by the horses, he hadn't noticed that the sun had risen hot as a brand. The day would be more like August than early October.

"Indian summer."

"I hope it will last until November . . . when I leave."

"Might," Max said, but his mind wasn't on November. Something about today didn't feel right, and he peered over his shoulder at it as though he could feel something coming up behind him.

Max wiped imaginary sweat from his forehead with his sleeve. "You wanted to ride Lady. I'll be checking stock and fences this morning. Might be you'd like to come along."

"That I would."

"Better get some trousers. No sidesaddles within five hundred miles of here. And wear my Sunday boots. They won't fit, but you can't ride barefoot."

Max had the horses saddled when Catherine returned from the dugout. He explained the basics: mounting and dismounting, neck reining, heels and knees, and then stood back to watch the show.

Catherine was a natural rider. She sat astride Lady with the easy grace with which she did everything, back straight as a soldier's. The mare seemed to sense the spectacle she and her rider created, and she stepped a bit higher, head held even more regally than usual.

When Max nosed the stud north, Catherine pulled up beside him, and they rode that way, neither speaking to the other, each immersed in the magic of the moment.

They crossed the eastern shoulder of the ridge and then turned west, holding close to patches of shadow hugging the rimrock. The day had become almost intolerably hot, and there was tension in the air, a sense of expectancy.

They were following game trails carved over hundreds of years by the hooves of deer, elk, antelope, and buffalo. Now only deer and an occasional antelope used the path, and Max noticed few tracks of either animal. Some predator was working the ridge, and then as though to confirm his suspicions, he spotted the tracks of a wolf, padding its way through the soft soil at the bottom of a gully.

Max pointed out the tracks to Catherine and promised himself he would lace some deer guts with poison. Wolves don't make good winter neighbors.

The cattle were fat and scattered, seeking shade in the lee of trees and ledges strewn over the prairie. The four-strand, barbwire fence shone in the sun like a spider's web, and the springs were full and clear, pocked at the edges with the tracks of cattle and game.

Max wiped his forehead with his sleeve. Something was wrong, and he couldn't put his finger on it. The wind was picking up, but not the dry wind that haunts the prairie in the fall, shaking the last bit of life from grass and bushes. This wind didn't blow the earth stinging into the rider's eyes. Instead, the soil seemed anchored, waiting.

They were nearly to the west end of the hills when Max heard a low rumble in the distance. He nudged the stud into a trot until they broke free of the western shoulder of the rim. Off to the southwest lay a wall of black, broken occasionally by the flash of lightning.

"Storm coming up," Max said. "We'd best get back. You up to a gallop?" Catherine nodded, and Max put his heels to the stud.

He watched the storm out of the corner of his eye as they flew toward the dugout. It was too late for a thunderstorm like this in Montana, and it had been too hot today for this time of year. And then there was the rain, a whole week of rain. Something wasn't right, and Max didn't know what it was.

He reined the stud to a stop by the wagon and waited for Catherine to join him. Her face was flushed from the ride, and she wore the same expression she had that first day in the swing. Catherine seemed reluctant to climb down.

"Gather up what counts most for you, and put it in that trunk of yours. I'll put the horses in the barn and be back in a minute to help you get it up to the wagon."

Catherine's face shone. "Are you then going to set me free?"

"Can't talk, now. Hurry! Hurry!"

Max wheeled the horses and ran them to the barn. He opened the door, shooed Lady inside, and then dropped off the edge to the creek bottom, returning a few moments later with the mare and Percherons. He drove them into the barn and led the stud inside, leaving a moment later with a rolled-up tarp under his arm.

By the time he reached the dugout, Catherine had her trunk packed. She was wondering which dress she should wear to Prairie Rose, when Max burst through the door.

"Best get moving," he said, slamming the lid of the trunk.

Catherine's anger surged. "I'm not ready, and I will thank you to keep your hands off my things."

Max ignored her. He draped the tarp over the trunk and lifted it, the tendons of his neck and shoulders straining from the load.

"Shut the door on the way out."

Catherine's lip curled, and she stalked to the entrance. Mr. Maxwell Bass was about to get another lesson in manners. But when Catherine stepped outside, Max was gone. The sky had gone black, and the cottonwood was bowing to a wind exercising its dominion over the prairie. Max must be on top. Catherine climbed the hill, hearing the rumble of thunder off to the southwest.

Max was under the wagon. He had spread the tarp on

the ground and placed the trunk on it. He glanced at Catherine and then trotted toward the dugout, calling over his shoulder, "Climb under the wagon. I'll be back in a minute." He disappeared in a cloud of dust running ahead of the wind.

Catherine stood beside the wagon. She could see no earthly reason to crawl under it. She hesitated a moment and then marched toward the dugout, only to meet Max on his way back. Without a word, he grabbed her arm and tugged her toward the wagon. She struggled, and the two fought each other silently on a battleground of wind and dust while thunder rumbled like artillery in the background.

Catherine battled Max to a standstill until he reached down and encircled her waist with his arm, carrying her to the wagon.

Max threw his rifle on the tarp and turned his full attention to Catherine. He trapped her arms at her sides and kneeled. She was lying on her back, eyes stung with dust, helpless as a child, and for one long moment she was afraid that Max intended to rape her. Perhaps he was taken by the electricity in the air, the rumble of thunder that grew closer and closer by the moment, the flashes of lightning crashing down upon the earth.

But once he had Catherine under the wagon, Max turned his attention to other matters. He pulled the canvas over their backs for shelter, and they awaited the storm in swirls of dust, the canvas snapping over their heads in the wind.

The storm marched in like an army following a celestial barrage, God hurling bolts and rage upon the earth.

The day was black as night, lit only by threads of light. The bursts burned instant images on the eye: the cottonwood poking from a cloud of dust, the ridge ominous in blue-white and black. The earth heaved, and it seemed that the day of judgment had arrived.

And then Max was shouting in Catherine's ear, and she couldn't hear him above the shriek of the wind and the crash of the thunder, and then one word—"chickens"—and she was left alone on the tarp. The wind had picked up, and Catherine wondered whether her weight and the trunk could hold down the tarp or if it would billow like a sail and carry her away.

Her eyes searched for Max, and they caught him, here and then there. He seemed frozen in the flashes of lightning, only darkness and the crack and rumble of thunder pushing him toward the creek. The lightning outlined him leaning against the wind, and one bolt struck so close that Catherine thought he had been killed. But the next light revealed him just as he stepped over the edge of the hill on the way toward the chicken pen.

Catherine was alone in the midst of a heavenly barrage, the sole focus of God's power and anger, and she cringed deeper into the folds of the tarp. The electricity in the air tugged at her hair, and the nape of her neck crawled. And then Max appeared suddenly beside the wagon, a tin soldier on an Empyrean field. Just as he settled in beside her and pulled the tarp around himself, the first drops of rain sprayed against the wagon like rifle fire.

"Here it comes!" Max shouted, and Catherine's nerve almost broke. If what to come was worse than what had been, it was a matter of great dread, indeed.

The rain settled the dust, and the sky was not so dark as it had been. And then the torrent came. Rain fell in sheets, blocking everything but itself from the eye, flowing in over the edge of the tarp to drench Max and

Catherine. She started to rise, but Max grabbed her arm, and together they sat, wet from the bottom up in a freshwater sea deep as the clouds. And then the sea turned to ice. Hail, sporadic at first, peppered the land, rattling against the wagon box like shrapnel.

But Catherine wasn't watching the hail. A chicken freed by Max and terrified by the storm ran in circles in a futile attempt to escape the hail. One pellet struck her at the juncture of the neck and body, and she turned belly up, feet clawing vengeance on the storm that had killed her.

The storm rolled past, and Catherine watched it go, wondering at the terror it would strike downwind, wondering how many dead and twisted creatures it would leave in its wake. Max crawled from beneath the wagon. Catherine was sitting in a little curl on the canvas, and he offered her his hand, but she ignored him. Max took her arm, and she struggled against him instinctively, much as the chicken had clawed at the storm.

The hair on the back of her neck crawled. The air crackled still with electricity, and she felt exposed, as though she were standing in the presence of God.

"Why did you drag me out in that?" she whispered. "Why didn't you let me sit that out in the dugout? We could have been killed."

"Storm came in from the southwest," Max said as he led her toward the bank overlooking the dugout. "Same as the creek drainage."

When Max released her arm and stepped ahead to spread the tarp again on the ground, Catherine said, "Mr. Bass, if there is more to this show, I don't want to see it."

"We don't have much choice."

When Catherine reached the lip of the hill, she understood. Pishkin Creek was over its banks, brown as the wheat field and wild as a mountain stream. It surged against the sandstone wall on the other side as though it intended to break that stricture and roar out on the prairie, claiming the land once again for its own.

The creek was eight feet above its banks and only four feet below the entrance to the dugout, and it was rising by the moment.

Catherine was taken with the sheer power of the flood, appalled at the death it paraded past. A two-year-old steer twisted and turned in the current until it lodged against the cottonwood, mouth open in a macabre grin at the spectacle it created. Here and there, an animal struggled still against the flood and death.

And then near the other side of the creek was a rattlesnake, head high, writhing through the water, then two and three and four and more.

"Must have gotten into a den," Max said, rising to return to the wagon. He came back, jacking a shell into the rifle. He sat down a short distance from Catherine and fired into the stream, and Catherine wasn't sure if he was shooting at the snakes or at the creek.

But the creek seemed to take umbrage. It reared up, riding a wall of water broken loose from Max's earthen dam upstream. The logs he had buried in the dam had washed loose and were bumping their way down the creek.

One of the logs, longer than a telegraph pole, poked through the back of the swing and lodged. The current swung the other end, *thump,* against the trunk of the cottonwood like a battering ram. Then the creek raged against the log as it raged against anything that slowed its wild ride downstream. The tree groaned and twisted with the burden.

"Shallow roots," Max said in answer to a question that had not been asked. "Cottonwoods have shallow roots. Doesn't take much sometimes to push them over."

Max picked up his rifle and began firing at the log—slugs splintered the wood, leaving patches of yellow and gray bobbing down the creek. Then he changed his aim, loud *clangs* marking the times his slugs found the chain that held the swing to the tree.

But in the end, Max laid his rifle on the tarp. This battle was between forces beyond his control. The creek had fed and watered the cottonwood for a hundred years. If the bill had come due, the cottonwood would pay it.

Max's hands needed something to do. He rose and walked to the chicken, lying now in a melting mound of hail. He picked up the bird and twisted her head off so she would bleed out as he carried her back to the tarp. There, he opened her with his pocketknife, reaching into her body cavity and pulling her guts free. He stood and threw the entrails, writhing through the air like snakes into the creek.

"You missed one," he muttered to himself, kneeling at a puddle and rinsing his hands of the blood and stench.

"Now, we've got something to eat if we can find somewhere to eat it." Max nodded at the steps leading into the dugout. The water was lapping at the last one, only inches away from the bottom of the door. Max turned his attention to the cottonwood and the swing he had hung from it and the flood that was trying to push the tree out of its way.

"It took my hay," he said. "All we've got left is what's in the loft. This is my fault. I was bragging about having hay, about beating this country. You rear up on your hind legs like that, and you get slapped down."

"Should I bow to you?"

Max's eyebrows knotted.

"I've never been in the presence of a man so important," Catherine said, "that God would subject the rest of us to a storm like that just to humble him."

Max's eyes disappeared into thin slits. He looked at Catherine as he had looked at the flood moments before, but whatever he was about to say was interrupted by a groan and crash from the creek. Pressure behind the log had finally become unbearable, and the swing had broken—almost burst.

As Catherine watched the log shake itself loose from the tree, she remembered the first day she had seen the swing, the promise it had held for her, and the despair she felt when she learned the truth. Her mind was playing with that as she heard the sound of a galloping horse behind her.

It was one of the Lenington boys: Andrew, she thought. Water sprayed from the horse's hooves as the boy made his way to them. The horse slipped and almost fell as he pulled the animal to a stop.

"Ma wants you to come quick as you can. Little Joey's lost in the creek."

Catherine sucked in her breath. She remembered Joey from the barn raising, hanging from the ledge across the creek, fighting Edna's grasp to go into the circle of children to face the rattlesnake again.

"I want to go," she said.

"Might as well," Max said. "If your eyes are half as sharp as your tongue, you'll be the one to spot him."

Catherine ignored Max's jibe in her rush to the barn for Lady.

The Toomey place was already teeming with neighbors as Max and Catherine rode up. Klaus was standing lost and alone in the middle of more people than most of them had seen since the barn raising.

Nobody seemed to be paying much attention to him: They were all busy with the search. Some of the men had ropes tied around their waists and were wading chest deep in the creek, feeling with their feet for Joey's body. Occasionally, the current would upset one man or another and he would be swept downstream until the crowd on the bank could drag him to shore, wet and dripping like a big fish.

The children, left to entertain themselves, eddied and swirled about the homestead, never free of one mother's eyes or another. And in the eyes of each of those women was relief that her child had not been the one taken and guilt for feeling that way.

One of the men from the barn raising—Catherine couldn't remember his name—stepped up to Max.

"Klaus thinks Joey went in down there. He was playing by the creek, and then he was gone. Long slide mark by the water. Feet probably went out from under him. We figure he caught up in that barbwire downstream, and the current held him under until he drowned.

"Klaus was in the tack shed oiling harness when it happened. Doesn't know how long Joey's been gone. He hightailed it to the Leningtons for help, and he's been standing there ever since like he's to blame."

The man hesitated, looking off toward the creek where the other men were wading in the cold, muddy water, and then he spoke. "There's some who say he is to blame. He never was one to pay much attention to the boy."

Catherine was thinking about the towhead at the barn raising, trying so hard to be part of the children's play without knowing how. So Joey had played with death, and now death had called him, and the little boy had followed the only real companion he had ever had.

"Maybe the water just carried him downstream?"

"We've been half a mile down, ma'am, watching both sides real careful. Not a sign of him. If he's downstream, he's probably halfway to North Dakota by now."

"I'm going downstream," Catherine said.

"Think I'll go along," Max said, and the two edged over to the creek bank.

The men were wading the creek to find Joey's body. The only hope of finding Joey alive was downstream.

Catherine didn't know if she expected to find the boy or just needed to flee from his dead-eyed father, terrified at the thought that she might have to watch Klaus's face as the men placed Joey's body in his arms.

"They're shunning him, aren't they?" she asked as they rode away.

"Maybe," Max said. "Maybe he's shunning himself."

The creek raged still, chocolate brown from chunks of soil torn from above. Most of the animals caught in the creek bottom were already dead, washed against some outcropping of plant or rock. But here or there a ground squirrel or a prairie dog shivered atop some high point, waiting to be dried by the sun and for the creek to go down.

At one point, they came upon a bobcat so intent with the harvest of dead and near-dead animals along the creek that he didn't notice Max and Catherine until they were directly behind him. He hissed and leaped into the flood, swimming expertly for the other side.

They had long passed the half-mile mark where the

other searchers had scuffed the earth with their heels before turning back, when Max pulled the stud to a halt. "Not much sense going beyond here. We aren't going to find him downstream. Probably won't find him at all until the water goes down. Best I can do now is go back with the other men wading the creek. Doesn't take long in that water to shake the warm out."

"No!" Catherine said, her head canted and shaking. She looked at Max from the corner of her eye. "No! You go back if you want to. I'm going to find Joey."

Max reached out to touch Catherine's shoulder, but pulled back. His voice was low and restrained: "It's tough, but there's nothing we can do about it. If you want to look, look, but stay back from the edge, and if you see him . . . in the water, let him go. Pulling him out isn't worth dying for."

Catherine's face was white, and she wouldn't look at Max, her eyes fixed on Lady's ears. She tried to speak, but her mouth moved soundlessly, and finally she turned Lady downstream and began her search.

Max was walking the stud back to the Toomey place, torn between the need to pitch in—to give his mind and body a task to occupy them—and his need to watch over Catherine. He stopped and turned just in time to see Catherine and Lady disappear over the edge of the bank toward the flood.

He wheeled the stud and kicked the horse into a gallop. They sped toward the edge, mud flying in chunks big as tea saucers.

Max was a cautious man. But he wasn't thinking about caution now: He was thinking about Catherine, and as he neared the creek bank, he touched his heels to the horse's sides and the stud jumped. The two sailed over the edge, neither knowing what awaited them below.

Catherine had been walking the horse along the bank, her eyes seeking some shape, some color that didn't fit the edges and surface of the flood. She had stopped for a moment, tears blurring her vision, when she caught movement from the corner of her eye. She blinked until her eyes cleared. There was a raft of driftwood across the creek. And on the outside edge flickered a patch of white almost as pale as the bleached wood, but different somehow. And as Catherine watched, another patch of white swirled out of the water, and on the end of it was a sleeve!

Catherine reined Lady toward the creek, and the two slid down the bank, the mare scrambling to find footing. They plunged into the flood, and Catherine gasped with the shock of the cold water.

The mare was swimming across and down, and Catherine turned the animal's nose more into the current, trying to make up the distance they were losing to the flood.

They touched the bank on the other side below the driftwood and tried to climb up, but the bank was too steep and slick. Lady fought the bank and the water and her fear, and Catherine took those few desperate moments to kick her foot out of the stirrup on the downstream side. She jerked her leg over the horse and jumped one-legged for the bank.

She landed chest first, and the impact knocked the wind from her. She was sucking air, but her lungs came up empty, and she thought she would suffocate. And as she gasped for breath, the current pushed her legs toward the mare's flailing hooves. Her wind caught about the same time her hand brushed through a patch of silver sage. She held on, her breath coming in sobs.

Catherine pulled herself to her hands and knees and then stood, balancing precariously at the edge of the creek. Lady was scrambling wild-eyed to climb the bank, but Catherine knew the horse would die in the trying. She slipped off Lady's bridle.

"Git! Git!"

Lady swung into the current and was gone. The banks were steep on both sides, and Catherine knew there was little chance the horse would find sanctuary before her strength gave out. Just as that reality was drumming into her mind, Max and the stud appeared in midair. They struck the creek, *WHOOSH!* Then the horse disappeared, leaving only Max's head and shoulders visible before he vanished in a sheet of spray.

When Catherine had blinked her eyes clear, Max was almost across the creek, the impetus of the jump giving the stud a better start than the mare. Above the drift pile, there was a rock ledge that poked hidden into the creek, and the stud clambered on top and stood knee deep in the water.

Max climbed down slowly. He stood, talking softly until the stud's eyes stopped rolling. Then Max stepped quietly away. As he approached Catherine, his eyes were as wild as the horse's had been. "What the hell happened?"

"He's in the driftwood, there."

Max's eyes searched the area where Catherine was pointing and came up empty. Then he saw the upper half of the boy's face thrust up and back out of the water. Max had dreaded the prospect of finding the child's body. He hated the thought of pulling Joey's corpse from the water, carrying it back to Klaus, who was standing in a pool of guilt amidst his neighbors' accusing eyes. Max hesitated a moment before stepping out on the driftwood.

"Hurry!" Catherine cried.

"No need. Won't make any difference to him."

"He's alive. I saw him raise his arm out of the water."

"Just the current. Makes him seem like he's moving, but it's just the current."

But as Max watched, Joey's arm rose slowly from the water until it was extended nearly full length. It waved weakly for a moment, and then fell back with a splash.

"I'll be damned," Max muttered as he edged out to the head of the driftwood. He reached under the water and grabbed Joey by the shoulders.

Joey struggled weakly, but the boy was exhausted. The effort of holding his nose above water against the weight and cold of the flood had drained him of all the reserves stored in his little body. He was near death, but still he struggled.

Max looked up. "I'll need some help. Have to reach under to find what he's caught on. You hold his head up in case something slips."

As Catherine crept toward the two, balancing on bits of driftwood thrust up from the pile, Max cautioned, "Easy. This is like standing on a bag of marbles, and if it slips we're all gone."

But the warning wasn't needed. A moment before, Catherine had stepped on a loose log and slipped into water waist deep before finding solid footing. She was moving slowly and tentatively now.

When Max felt her hands over his, he reached down, seeking the snag that held the boy tight. Joey's left cuff was twisted into a broken branch, and Max tugged until the sleeve split, and Joey's face bobbed free from the water. Still the driftwood held Joey in a grip tight as death.

"Something deeper," Max said, ducking under the water.

Above water, the flood roared as though outraged at the limits imposed on it by rocks and banks and a little boy's body. But below, the stream chattered at Max with the clicks and rattles of stones racing each other downstream. The flood seemed to be calling him to add his bones to the race, hungry for another life to spit up on the bank, and a chill ran through his body.

Joey's foot was pinched between two logs, and Max came out of the water gasping for breath.

"He's pinned. When I try to break him loose, the whole shebang could go and us with it."

Max scrambled up the drift toward the stud. When he returned a moment later, he handed Catherine one end of a rope. "Tie it around your waist. No slack or it might get tangled. If the driftwood lets go, hang on to Joey. The current should swing you into the bank."

Max didn't tell Catherine that if the logs shifted the wrong way, Joey's foot could be crushed or pinched off at the ankle. But there were no options. If he wasn't released and soon, he would die. The boy was nearly comatose from the killing cold of the water. Already, Joey had hung to a tenuous thread of life longer than Max thought possible.

He tugged a chokecherry pole thicker than his arm and taller than he was from the driftwood and ducked under again. The flood nagged at him as his hands explored Joey's foot and the logs that imprisoned it, and finally Max was satisfied.

"Pray for us, Catherine," he said and hung his weight and strength and life on the end of the pole. Solid! The damn thing was solid! Those two logs were probably the foundation for the whole pile, buried under the weight of the other logs and the power of the flood.

Max braced his feet and leaned again into the pole. The muscles of his shoulders and back and legs bulged under the pressure, and Catherine could read the strain on his face more clearly than a book. She grabbed Joey's shirt with one hand, holding his lolling head above water with the other. Then she leaned into the pole, putting her fear and hope and strength into the effort, and slowly, inexorably, the logs in the pile began to move. Max could hear them groaning in protest, but they moved and the drift pile shifted just a bit . . . and Joey popped free.

Catherine was holding Joey to her breast and sobbing, and her tears triggered Max's own. The three of them made their way across the drift pile like that, Catherine sobbing and tears blurring Max's vision. For the first time in his life, Max didn't care if someone saw him cry.

They stood for a moment on the bank, holding Joey between them, sharing the warmth of their bodies with the boy, arms encircling each other. Catherine looked up at Max, her tear-streaked face shining as though she had seen the rapture, and Max kissed her. Catherine kissed him back, and Max felt as though he could walk across the flood, carrying Catherine and Joey to safety.

But that thought broke the mood: There was still more to be done. Joey's lips and fingernails were blue with the cold; they had to get the boy back to the cabin or he would die. They couldn't scramble up the rain-soaked bank above them, with the stud or without. The only hope lay downstream, and that hope was slim indeed. The creek might wind for miles between steep, slick banks. If they didn't find a way out they would drown. But there was nothing to do but to trust fate.

Max led Catherine to the stud, helping her into the saddle.

"You take the boy. Give the horse his head unless he panics and heads for a bank he can't climb. I'll be behind you. Might be you could wait a minute to toss me the rope as I come by."

Catherine's question was plain on her face.

"Can't swim," Max said. He toppled a log off the driftwood and into the flood and plunged after it. The stud caught Max a few moments later, and Catherine reached for him from the saddle.

Max waved her away. "That horse gets too close, he'll kick me to death and spill you into the creek. This will work out. You take care of Joey. I'll do fine."

They bobbed down the flood together for a few moments, a tiny flotilla of life on a thread of death snaking its way across the Montana prairie. And then the stud pulled away, swimming strongly. Catherine twisted in the saddle to watch Max, only his head showing behind the log. His eyes were focused on her as though he wanted to keep her image etched forever on his mind, and he waved good-bye as she disappeared behind the first curve in the creek.

Catherine held Joey tight. There seemed to be only a spark of life left in the boy, and she fanned that with the warmth of her body. But she sought comfort in the embrace, too. As they moved down the creek, surrounded on both sides by high, insurmountable banks, Gentleman's Promise was beginning to blow with the effort of swimming, and Catherine shuddered.

But their only hope lay ahead, not behind, and on they went, the sky blue and clear above, the sun warm on their backs, and death waiting coldly below for the horse to finally tire and panic.

Then Catherine saw the stud's ears go forward, and he began swimming for the bank. She tried to pull the horse's head downstream. But for the first time in his life, he fought the bridle, and Catherine panicked. If the stud reached the bank and tried to scramble up, she and Joey would die under his hooves or be thrown back to be claimed by the flood.

So Catherine fought the stud silently, matching will to will and strength to strength, and then she heard a whinny over the roar of the creek. Perhaps one of the searchers had come looking for them. Perhaps death was not yet inevitable. So she hugged Joey even tighter and gave Gentleman's Promise his head. She could feel the horse's hooves churning faster as he swam toward the curve ahead and whatever lay beyond.

Max's body hung behind the log like a sea anchor. He felt weightless, borne by a cold, raging wind down a world defined by the high banks of Pishkin Creek and a ribbon of sky above. That wind was cold, and Max was shivering. Despite his weightlessness, his arms were tired with the strain of tying his body to the log, to life. He wanted to shift his grip, but his hands were numb, and he wasn't sure he could will them to let go or to grasp again. He seemed to be sinking deeper, and the strain of holding his face above water made hard, stiff lines of the tendons of his neck. And finally, Max draped his arms over the log, flexing his hands to bring warm blood and strength to them, hoping the log wouldn't roll and leave him to drown. And he fought his mind as he fought the cold. It would be so easy to let go. No one could blame him for that. But Max wouldn't give up. Not yet.

As they rounded the curve, Catherine could see a break in the bank marking the course of a smaller, feeder stream. There was a small meadow there half-covered by water, and at the head of the meadow stood Lady. She had been cropping grass beside the creek, but as the flood-runners appeared, the mare raised her head to nicker. The stud surged toward shore, carving a V into the water, and Catherine felt the horse's hooves strike ground. As they neared shore, the current shifted, moving back upstream as though the flood were a child, anxious to take one more wild ride before moving on. A moment later, they were standing beside the mare, the stud's sides heaving with exhaustion.

It was warm in the meadow, cut off from the wind and open to the full weight of the sun. Catherine steadied Joey on the saddle and stepped down, lifting the boy from the horse. Joey was limp, and Catherine carried him, supporting his head with one hand as though he were an infant, to a rock that poked out of the bank on the northern edge of the meadow. She stripped him, and laid him on the warm rock, lifeless as a basket of wash hung out to dry.

She was wringing the boy's clothing when one of the horses nickered: Max had just rounded the curve. He had spotted the meadow and was trying to push the log toward it, but the log had more substance than he, and he was swimming only weakly.

Catherine dropped Joey's clothes and ran to the stud. The horse shied, dancing until Catherine caught the reins. She jerked the rope free from the saddle and ran toward Max, copper water spraying silver from her feet.

If she couldn't put the rope in his hands, he would be swept downstream to die while she raced keening along the bank above, watching helplessly.

She threw. Short! The rope snaked back to her in arm-length jerks. She twirled it over her head and let it fly again. It sailed past Max, but as it came full length, it jerked back and fell across the log. Max slipped the loop over his head and under one arm, and the rope tightened, and he was yanked off the log. Max had every nonswimmer's fear of being in water over his head, and he kicked and slapped at the flood, fighting panic, fighting to keep his face above water.

Catherine was pulled off her feet by Max's weight and the power of the flood, and she was being drawn toward deep water and death. If she let go, she could save her own life and Joey's, but she couldn't do that. She had begun a litany of Holy Marys, and then she spotted a dead juniper sticking about six inches above the surface of the water. She pulled, kicked and swam to that pole and looped the rope around it. Max swung heavy on the end of the line, and the rope cut into his chest and neck until he thought he would be strangled. Odd, he thought, to hang yourself so you wouldn't drown. But as he swung toward shore, his body was caught in the eddy drifting back upstream. Catherine could pull him along, then, taking in the slack with half hitches around the juniper stump, and finally he was there.

Max's arm came from the water, and he grabbed the juniper in the crook of his arm, embracing it as though it were life itself. They stood there, in chest-deep water, looking into each other's eyes and gasping for breath.

"Catherine O'Dowd," Max said. "You're one hell of a woman. If you weren't married, I'd ask you to tie up with me."

"And if I weren't married," Catherine said, her voice so soft Max could just hear it over the roar of the flood, "I might have said yes."

"Yeah?" Max said, wiping his forehead with his sleeve. "Joey all right?"

"We have to get him back and get him warmed up."

Max drew a deep breath. "I'll take the rope and wade into shallower water. You leave it tied until I get set. Then I'll give you a hand coming in."

The crowd at the Toomey place had swelled in the hour, year, century they had been gone. The women had a table heaped with food. There was a bonfire roaring in front of the cabin, and some of the men who had been wading the creek looking for Joey's body were circled around it, blankets draped over their heads and open at the front to catch the heat, celebrants of an ancient rite.

Klaus hadn't moved. He stood alone in a crowd of milling people, hat held across his chest, eyes fixed on the thin line that defines sky and land in Montana.

Children were scattered through the scene like pepper in a pot, and one spotted Joey. Wonder chased surprise from his face, and he ran for the dugout, shouting at the top of his voice: "They got Joey! They got Joey! They got Joey!"

All eyes turned to the creek in dread.

"No, there," the boy shouted, pointing to Max and Catherine, "and he's alive."

A shout went up from the crowd, and the homesteaders pushed singlemindedly toward the riders. People were shouting and talking and pointing to Joey, clapping one another on the back and wiping tears away with aprons and sleeves.

Klaus looked up at Catherine, his face ravaged by tears strong enough to crack a rock, and when he spoke it was as though he were reciting a high and holy prayer.

"I'm sorry, Joey. I'm sorry, Joey. I'm sorry, Joey."

Klaus reached for Joey and held him tight to his breast, his breath coming in choking sobs. And then, tentatively, two little four-year-old arms reached around his father's neck, and the cheer from the crowd must have been heard in heaven.

Max and Catherine rode to the homestead in silence. They stopped at the dugout, and Max went inside to pull blankets and pillows from the bed. Catherine's trunk was still sitting under the wagon, and she picked a change of clothing from that.

They left the door to the dugout open, and the dry fall air pulled moisture from the raw earth like a wick. After Max cared for the horses, he pitched hay into one of the unused stalls and spread his bedroll there. Then he carried Catherine's bedding into the loft. As he came downstairs, she was looking out the barn door, seeing in her mind's eye the tears on Toomey's face and little Joey's hug, perhaps his first.

"Maybe I was wrong," Catherine said, smiling at Max. "Perhaps God did call this storm upon us for a reason."

CHAPTER 14

CATHERINE awoke to the scent of hay and fresh-cut pine. She had grown accustomed to the dugout—air heavy as earth and raw as a wound—and by comparison the hayloft seemed light and easing to her spirit.

Max's snoring below had awakened her several times during the night, and she had heard him leave the barn some time ago. She dressed in the dark and made her way to the ladder leading from the loft, climbing down through shadow into the light of a kerosene lantern, painting the barn in yellows, browns, and blacks. She picked her way through the light to the door outside.

Max was sitting in a globe of flickering yellow light cast by a campfire, and Catherine wondered for a moment where he had found dry wood after yesterday's storm. The sky was glorious, stars bright enough to tug at the soul. She stood in the midst of infinity and felt exalted, not humbled, for her small part in something so vast and beautiful.

Max had carried the table and chairs from the dugout to the campfire, and Catherine took hers, watching him as he cut bacon.

"Mud's ankle deep in the root cellar, and the ice is gone," Max said. "Bacon was hanging from the ceiling, and water doesn't hurt potatoes so they're all right. Everything else is gone."

"What about the dugout?"

"Water got in, but not too bad. Don't go in yet,

though. The whole thing might just drop into the creek."

"It's good we got the trunk out."

Max nodded.

"Max?" Catherine said tentatively. "Yesterday was special, but it doesn't change anything. I'm still leaving when Father Tim comes."

"It changed one thing," Max said. "Catherine."

Catherine nodded, and Max smiled. "I like the sound of it."

The bacon and potatoes were done, and Max served breakfast on a table lit by the campfire and the stars. They lingered over coffee until the sun rose in the east, casting long shadows across the prairie of man, woman, and table.

They rose, then, walking together to the bank overlooking the creek. The water had retreated during the night, but the flood had strewn its bones across the bottom. There was silt and driftwood and carcasses from one high-water mark to the other. Catherine could hear the breath hissing through Max's teeth as he viewed the desolation.

The day was backbreaking. Catherine rode the creek, looking for live animals mired in the bottom, while Max cleaned up around the dugout. A section of corral fence had been torn down by the flood. The outhouse was leaning on its side, and the creek had filled the hole with silt. The chicken coop was gone, and much of the grass on the creek bottom was covered with mud. He had counted on the creek bottom for winter grass, and now it was gone. He felt like a man going into a Montana winter without a coat.

Max was a practical man. He built his days on a framework of priorities, working first to last. But today as he looked at the desolation across the bottom, his mind returned most frequently to the swing he had built for Catherine, and when she returned, it was the swing he was working on.

She watched for a moment, a shadow crossing the pensive smile on her face, and then she took Lady back to the barn and unsaddled her.

They spent the next three days picking up after the flood. They butchered one steer they found, hanging it spread-eagled and obscene from the cottonwood. The owner offered them half the beef for their trouble, but they had no place to keep the meat, so they settled on one loin and ate steak and roast at their prairie table until it was gone.

Just as Catherine grew accustomed to the barn and eating by starlight, Max declared the dugout safe. They pulled out the canvas floor, scrubbed it in the creek and hung it to dry on the south wall of the barn.

And on their first night underground, they sat in the light of the kerosene lamp, eating the last of the loin steak. Max leaned back from the table picking at his teeth with a splinter from the kindling pile. Then he leaned forward, took his coffee cup, and whispered, "We're being watched."

Catherine jerked, her eyes probing the shadows that lay beyond the reach of the lamp's circle of yellow light.

"How can we be watched?" she whispered. "A man would have to be buried in the wall to watch us here."

"I didn't mean that," Max whispered. "I meant there is a man outside watching."

"How can he watch us inside if he's outside?" Catherine muttered, irritation creeping into her voice.

"I didn't say he was watching us inside," Max hissed.

"Then by all that's holy, why are we whispering?"

"Sshhhh! He might be listening."

Catherine's eyes flashed, and with every word her voice crept up the musical scale. "Maxwell Bass, I have long thought that you have only a tenuous grip on your senses, and now you have lost even that. . . ."

Catherine was reaching for high C when Max cut in again, "Sshhhh!"

The muscles in Catherine's jaw knotted, and she spoke through clenched teeth, "Don't you sshhhh me!"

They glared at each other from across the table, eyes in slits, blood flooding their faces red.

"I'm sorry," Max whispered, "but we are being watched, and I'm afraid there may be someone listening to us this very moment."

Catherine's temper fled, and she looked at Max from the corner of her eyes. She was sitting in a dugout in the middle of the big empty with a man who believed that someone was eavesdropping on their conversation.

He leaned forward and whispered, "There's a willow bank about three hundred yards upstream. He lies up there during the day and watches us with binoculars. I saw the sun flash off the glass, and I found his tracks this morning going up to the stovepipe. He's been listening down the stovepipe."

Max's voice dropped even lower. "He's probably up there now."

"Who?"

"Don't know for sure, but you can bet the banker's in on it. Whoever he is has been digging holes, just like the banker did that night.

"Couldn't figure it out, at first. Found lots of holes dug all over the place. Seems clear to me that he's looking for the money, Catherine. Just like the banker."

Catherine's eyes narrowed as she sought some clue

that Max suspected she had betrayed him. But there was none. "What are we going to do about him?"

Indeed, that was the question.

Milburn Phillips pressed his ear to the stovepipe, waiting for that cowpoke to give away his treasure.

So far, the only fruit of his vigil were the stories he would tell cousin Aloysius. If he'd married a looker like the Bass woman he wouldn't spend his nights in the barn while she slept in the dugout. No, sir!

And the fights! Milburn had his ears blistered more than once, and it wasn't because the stovepipe was hot, either.

That cowpoke, Max Bass, just didn't know how to treat a lady, Milburn thought. No wonder she makes him sleep in the barn.

The current focus of Milburn's amorous intentions was a little beauty he had found in Ma Bovary's Liquor Emporium and House of the Gentle Arts.

The thought of her—blond hair, black eyes, a beauty mark that rotated from one cheek to the other, and a face hard enough to strike sparks—sent a quiver through his loins and drew his attention away from the pipe.

He had been true to her in the weeks before cousin Aloysius had called him to Prairie Rose—not going upstairs with any of the other women—but he had to admit that recently his thoughts had been pulled to Catherine as he watched her from the willow bank. Whoeee! Would he like to take her for a ride.

Phillips had been at the Bass place three days now, and those days had been hard on him. The right side of his face—his right ear was the good one—was stained black from the chimney. His hair had long since taken on a life of its own; it poked from his head here and there as though in some great jest, and his eyes were red-rimmed and wild.

But Milburn knelt singleminded on bunch grass and pressed his good ear against the stovepipe. Make believe about the Bass woman was fun, but money would buy him all the women a man could want. And after he had the money, Milburn could see no earthly reason to burden his cousin with that information. Aloysius already had a bankful.

Beneath him someone opened the door of the stove to put some more coal in. Good! He would be able to hear everything now.

Max tossed a couple chunks of coal on the fire and left the stove door open. Then he sat down across from Catherine, nodded, and took a sip of coffee from his cup.

She said loudly: "Max, I don't like leaving all that wheat money just lying around in here. Gone as much as we are, anyone could come in and take it."

"Yeah," he replied, equally loud, "suppose you're right. Best that I put it away."

"You're never going to tell me where you hide your money, are you?"

Max and Catherine's voices came through the stovepipe muffled and a little hard to understand, but Milburn was all grins as he listened. Those days of lying outside, ear pressed to this damn pipe, hadn't been pleasant, but they were about to pay off. Could be that he would be back at Ma Bovary's living the genteel life within the week.

He heard Max say, "Well, I suppose I could tell you

where the money is hidden. You promise to be especially careful?"

"Cross my heart."

"I hide it under water."

A thin line of spittle dripped from the corner of Milburn's mouth. There was something about the mention of money that made him drool.

"You hide it in the creek?" Catherine asked.

"Nope. I hide my gold and silver in watering holes. Other cowhands used to wonder why I always volunteered to clean out the springs and reservoirs, but I'd come back to the bunkhouse smug as can be and my pockets plumb full of gold."

Milburn was drooling out of both sides of his mouth now. The thought of pockets bulging with gold was almost sensual. He hugged the stovepipe tighter, and it shifted a bit, loosening a cloud of soot that sifted down on him like black snow. He fought a terrible urge to sneeze. He didn't want to miss a word.

Max's voice rumbled from the pipe, "What I do is poke the coins down in the mud, and they work their way down to bedrock. So when I want my money, I just start at the uphill side of a spring and dig down to bare rock and then work across. You leave one speck of mud on the bottom, it might be covering three, four double eagles."

Milburn swallowed. Aloysius had said Bass had five thousand dollars: That would be two hundred and fifty double eagles or five hundred eagles. A man couldn't carry that much money, no matter how big his pockets.

Max continued, "Happened a time or two that somebody would be digging in a spring and find one of my silver dollars. But they'd quit and never find the big money. Most of the time, it all works its way into one pocket, and you might dig the whole spring out before you find the coins."

Milburn shook his head, and it banged lightly against the pipe, loosening another cloud of soot. Not him. He wouldn't quit. He wouldn't quit until he had the whole five thousand dollars.

"I've got it all hidden in a spring up on the ridge. I'll show you where it is tomorrow, but we'll have to be careful. A man sitting above us on the rimrock could see the whole thing."

Milburn grinned. This thing was fitting together like a picture puzzle. He walked back to the willow bank to gather his bedroll, a little puff of soot marking each step he took. He'd be up on the ridge tomorrow morning when Max Bass and his new bride paid a visit to their bank. And as soon as they left, he'd slip down with the shovel and make himself a millionaire. Well, damn near a millionaire, anyway.

Milburn had spent the night on the bare rock that topped the ridge. A couple of nights ago, he wouldn't have been able to do that, the rock outlining the bones of his body in pain, but he was weary from nights spent slapping insects on the willow bank. In comparison, the cold night on the hard rock seemed like a night at Ma Bovary's.

He awoke before daylight, drifting between sleep and wakefulness until the sun stung his eyes open. Milburn rose, scratched day-old insect bites, and walked barefoot across the rim, wincing as his feet found sharp rocks, to a bush where he relieved himself.

He drank tepid, muddy water from the canteen and cut off a chunk of jerky, chewing hard and thinking about one of the big T-bones they served at the Stockman. Wouldn't be long now before he'd be back in Billings living like a king. He put the jerky and canteen back in the bag with his bedroll, and walked to the edge of the rim, stretching. Long way down to those rocks, and farther still to that Bass fellah and his woman riding up that little valley—whoops! He dropped to his knees and scrambled back. They must have seen him, sharp against the sky.

Milburn set his mind to the creation of a believable lie that would explain his presence on the rim. But his mind was as empty as his belly. He snaked forward for another look. His luck held: The Basses were still coming. Milburn grinned. Rubes they were, and rubes were no match for a man of the world like Milburn P. Phillips.

Max stood at the edge of the spring, the double eagle in his hand flashing yellow in the fall sun. Then he slipped the coin into the palm of his hand and threw a pebble he had concealed there into the spring. Replenishing his supply of rocks from his pockets, Max repeated the process: fifteen pebbles and four silver dollars.

Phillips watched the performance with the intensity of a zealot, a small pool of drool collecting on the rock under his chin. More than anything, he wanted to get into that spring with a shovel.

Milburn P. Phillips would become a wealthy man as soon as those honyockers stopped dilly-dallying around that little valley and gave a man a chance to go to work. Work—Milburn shuddered with aversion. But he would work today so that he could spend the rest of his life lying on a white beach in the south of France.

His mind turned to gentle, Mediterranean breezes stirring the revealing curtain dresses those French women wore shamelessly in public. Probably a lot of rubes there, too. Smart man like him might wind up with a castle. Let cousin Aloysius try to top that.

Max and Catherine had seen him silhouetted that morning like one of the redheaded buzzards that frequent southeastern Montana in summer. The trap had been laid but they had no way of knowing whether he had taken the bait.

After the chores were done and the chicken fried, Max saddled the two Appaloosas. Catherine came from the house in a light spring dress. On her head was the green hat from the Cole General Store, her hair spraying red-gold beneath it, and on her feet were Max's dress boots.

He was so taken with her beauty that a lump rose in his throat. He tried to tell her how he felt, but the words stuck, and he busied himself with the horses, trying to take his mind off Catherine.

They rode east as though they were going to town, but after they reached the fence line, they turned north and rode coulee bottoms back up to the northern edge of the ridge. It was cool in the shade of the hill, and Catherine shivered a bit. Max hobbled the horses and left them to graze in a swale of knee-high grass. They hiked up the steep flanks of the hill and scrambled through a break in the rock to the top of the rim, taking care not to kick any rocks loose.

Their concern was wasted. Phillips had already left his nest, a scattering of muddy blankets near the edge of the rim. Catherine and Max walked towards the blankets, crouching as they neared the rim.

Phillips was below, waist-deep in the muddy water of the spring, painfully pulling shovelful after shovelful of muck off the bottom of the spring, and depositing it on the bank.

"Have to give him credit," Max whispered. "He works awful hard for easy money."

Catherine grinned, and the two stepped back from the rim.

"Best that we let him finish," Max said. "Otherwise, he'll always wonder if we didn't scare him off before he tapped the mother lode. Something I want to show you, anyway."

Max led Catherine toward the western shoulder of the rim, moving slowly in deference to her loose boots.

Eons before, the point of the rim—a half-acre in size—had dropped away from the main slab of sandstone. Wind, water, heat and frost had widened the gap, smoothing the walls. And over the intervening years, creatures had picked their way up a rough trail on one wall of the gap, their hooves and pads and heels wearing the trail deeper.

Max took Catherine's hand and led her down the trail, into a chasm sixty feet deep, fifteen to twenty feet wide and only dimly lit by the fall sun.

Max pulled Catherine deeper into a chasm over a rough floor of shattered sandstone. Suddenly, he stopped and pointed up, and Catherine gasped. There, on the walls above her head, were pictographs, paintings by peoples long dead. There were pictures of men hunting bison, herds spilling over cliffs to their deaths, and strange creatures that looked like turtles. Max explained the figures represented men with large shields. Higher on the walls were pictures of warriors and long-necked horses.

Catherine walked captivated through the chasm, stopping now and then to trace fainter figures with her fingers, to wonder at the stories of long-dead people told with crude paints on stone.

"Who were they?" she whispered as though she were standing in a church.

Max shrugged. "Indians."

"How did they reach that high?"

"Stood on the backs of their horses." Max replied, pointing to a figure of a man standing on his horse, reaching above his head, colors spraying from his fingers.

They spent more than an hour in the chasm, until Catherine's mind was too filled with wonder to continue.

"What kind of people do you suppose they were?"

Max shrugged again. "Like us, I guess." He wiped his forehead with his sleeve. "Probably wanted to leave their mark on the land. Leave something to show they'd been here.

"Most of us would like that. Man can spend a lifetime out here and be gone with no more notice than someone blowing out a lamp. Most of us would like to leave something behind."

Catherine touched Max's sleeve. "Is that why you advertised for a wife?"

"Could be," Max sighed. "Could be that's the way it started, but that's not the reason I want you to stay. I . . . I . . . ," Max choked, and then hissed, "Damn me for a stiff-necked fool!" He wiped his brow with his sleeve. "We'd best get back. Just time to eat before he finishes the spring."

"Well look at this." Max jerked back from the rim, motioning for Catherine to join him.

The banker had joined Milburn at the spring, and the two men appeared to be arguing, bits and pieces of their dispute carried to Max and Catherine on vagrant winds.

Just as Catherine sat down, the banker launched a round-house swing at his cousin. Milburn, stiff still, tottered backward to escape the blow and fell full-length into the spring. The banker jumped after him, and the two scuffled, hampered in the battle by the resistance of the water and each man's deep desire not to be hurt.

"No honor among thieves," Max said. "Banker didn't figure he could trust his hireling and had to come looking. Makes it a lot easier for us. Let's go talk to our spies."

Milburn was covered to his armpits with the soft blue mud that lines the bottom of prairie springs, his face mottled red with sunburn where rivulets of sweat had washed away the soot. His lips were cracked and black with dried blood, and when he saw Max and Catherine riding up, he held his bloodied palms out, as though in supplication.

The banker, having spent less time bare-headed under the prairie sun, fared better. Blue with mud and fatter than Milburn, Aloysius appeared to be nothing so much as a primeval slug.

"Max," the banker said hastily when he saw he had been found out. "Glad you came along. Caught this scoundrel digging on your land, and tried to stop him." This slug was a fast thinker.

Milburn hissed. "Cousin, I'm not going to. . . ."

"Stop it!" Max's voice cut through the words like a cleaver. "I know why you're both here, and you'd best understand a couple of things before you go.

"First, there is no money except for the four dollars I

deliberately dropped in the spring. I figured it was worth that to get it cleaned out.

"Second, if I catch either of you on this place again, the next hole you dig will be the one you spend eternity in."

Max stepped off his horse and stomped toward the two, grabbing the retreating banker by the folds of fat on his throat.

"First thing you're going to do when you get back to Prairie Rose," he growled, "is tell those storekeepers that my credit is fine; that it was all just a joke."

Max's voice shook with rage. "And don't ever tell stories about my wife again!"

The banker shrank from the fire in Max's eyes, and Max gripped the skin on Aloysius's neck even tighter.

"This is big country out here," he whispered, menace poking from his words like rocks from a stream. "A man could take a drink in a bar and pass out and disappear, and nobody would think much about it.

"Do you know what I'm telling you?"

The banker, eyes big as dollars, tried to speak, but the best he could manage was "Uhhh-huhh."

"Now git!"

CHAPTER 15

THE sun was leaving the prairie, lingering longer some days than others, but there was no question of its intent.

Days were shorter: chores done and breakfast eaten in darkness. To step outside was to step into a raw wind—omen of winds to come—whispering its dominion over the prairie. Now it is my turn, it moaned soft as a lover; defy me if you dare, it screeched.

On those rare, warm days that grace Montana in the fall, Catherine found herself leaving the dugout and sitting in the wagon or swinging over the creek bottom carpeted in gold by the cottonwood.

There was a stillness, a sense of expectancy in the air, of impending change, and Catherine awaited November fourteenth and the arrival of Father Tim, her life in cusp.

The air crackled still as Max and Catherine came together, but not from rancor. They were more likely to laugh now than to quarrel.

Still when they might have pulled together, they pulled apart. November fourteenth loomed like a rock wall that sends a creek cascading down two sides of a mountain, one fork to the east and the other to the west.

Max and Catherine were pulling the roots that tied them together, so that when the parting came the pain would not be so great, but neither would admit that.

They talked, more than either had ever talked before to anyone, each sharing dreams and hopes, and they rushed together in the morning and lingered at night. But they also pulled back, leaving long, awkward silences whenever the talk touched chords too deep.

They had made one trip to Prairie Rose to fill their larder, and perhaps to assure themselves that life existed beyond the barbwire borders of the homestead.

Thomsen had come to see them one night. He had a part-time bartender he trusted, and he could slip away for a day without fidgeting to get back. They played cards and told stories and laughed. Mostly, they laughed.

The first snow had brought bitter cold. Wind kissed by ice fields to the north stung their faces numb. But like most fall storms in Montana, this one lasted only a week or so and then the snow melted, and the grass was carrying the cattle, fat into the winter.

They spent their days preparing for the cold. Max took Catherine to the coal outcropping in the southwest corner of the homestead and pried enough fuel from it with his pick to last the winter. They met several neighbors there with the same intent—and promises to pay Max later, or to drop a "little something" off at the Bass homestead around Christmas.

Max butchered a two-year-old steer and dropped a doe when she edged into his wheat field early one morning to nibble at the green winter wheat.

That meat, the potatoes in the restored root cellar and the hogs Zeb had promised to butcher, would take them into the winter in good shape.

Them.

Max couldn't—wouldn't—think about winter or spring or summer or next fall without Catherine. He knew that she intended to leave. He knew, too, that he wouldn't resist, but he couldn't bring himself to think about life without her.

Max had spent most of his life alone. Orphaned, he had come from Texas as a roustabout for a cattle drive. He couldn't remember his mother or his father, his only family being ranches where he had worked and friends he had picked up along the way.

Max had always prided himself on his self-reliance, but he had deep holes in his life that he yearned to fill with family. That was the root of his plot to capture Catherine, and now she intended to go and he would be alone again. He dreaded that.

He was thinking about that one cold morning as he and Catherine took the wagon to the Leningtons' to pick up their bacon and ham. They didn't talk, eager to see their friends. Except for the one trip to town, they had spent the past weeks in isolation.

The road to the Leningtons' was little more than two threads of dirt stitching big pieces of prairie together. Rutted, it was, with the weight of wagons and horses' hooves and broken by jutting rocks wherever the path crossed the slab of sandstone that underlay most of the region.

Max and Catherine rode, bobbing and weaving with the jolts of the wagon, silent and alone with their thoughts.

They smelled the Lenington place before they spotted it, riding a trail of wood smoke over the last rise to the cabin. Zeb was outside, peering into the smokehouse, gauging the depth and degree of "doneness" of the meat hanging there.

They saw Edna's face appear for a moment at the window, and then they caught only flashes of her, picking up around the house, making room for her visitors.

By the time Max had pulled the wagon to a stop, Edna had opened the door. She stood there, her hands tucking strands of hair into place.

"Come in! Come in! I was hoping you'd come today. Zeb says the ham is done to a fine turn, so you're just in time. Come sit. I've got coffee on, and I know Zeb will want you to try a slice of the ham. You know how he worries about it.

"Come on child!" she said, taking Catherine's arm. "No time for dawdling. Want to know everything you've been up to, and I've got some news for you, too."

The Lenington house was lived in, but neat by most standards—and temporarily empty. The children had disappeared in darkness that morning, waist deep in a wagonload of straw, blankets wrapped around their shoulders for warmth, bound for school. Without them, emptiness echoed through the house.

Cups of coffee were steaming on the table, and Edna dropped a couple chunks of coal in the Majestic range, sliding a cast-iron skillet on the stove to warm before Zeb appeared.

"Wait!" she said as Catherine and Max pulled chairs away from the table. "Zeb will want to show you his doings. Not fair to keep visitors all to myself. It'll only take a second, and he'll be so disappointed if you don't come out."

Zeb was already on his way to the house when Max, Catherine, and Edna stepped outside. He grinned. "As long as you're out, I might as well show you what I've been up to," he said, steering them toward the smokehouse.

Inside, slabs of bacon and hog shoulders and hams

hung from the ceiling in various states of curing. In the half light through eyes stung by acrid smoke, the scene was macabre.

"All honey cured," Zeb said proudly. "Montana honey's lighter than what I'm used to, and it puts a special kind of flavor to the meat. So sweet, you'd think you'd died and gone to—well, that's not up to me to say, is it?

"Come on inside. Maybe we can talk Edna into frying up a few pieces, and you can tell me what you think. It would be better baked, understand. But don't suppose you have time for that?"

Zeb cast a calculating eye on the two.

Max looked at Catherine. "Best be getting home. Got a ton of work to do before the fourteenth."

Max hadn't intended to mention the fourteenth. Although the date had occupied his mind for the past three weeks, neither he nor Catherine had spoken of it, neither wanting to open that wound.

"Fourteenth?" Edna asked. "What's going on the fourteenth?"

Then a grin crept on her face. "Should have known. Klaus is taking little Joey to Father Tim for baptism. I wouldn't miss that either. Not for the world."

Max and Catherine looked at each other, their faces barely masking the emotion beneath.

"We would like to see that," Catherine said, biting her lip.

"You'd better go," Edna said. "Klaus has been working on something special for you. I've seen it. It's a—don't suppose it hurts to tell you . . . he didn't say anything about not telling you—a cradle, all hand-carved and finished. He said he used to make cradles like that in the old country. He know something I don't?"

Catherine shook her head.

"Didn't think so. Anyhow, it's a beautiful thing. He said you gave life to his child. Said he wanted to do something for your children—when you have children.

"I'm making a quilt for the cradle. Hope you like it. Can't wait for you to see it. I'll show you the material."

Edna disappeared into her bedroom, emerging a moment later with two stacks of fabric pieces, one light blue and the other pink. "Thought I'd do it in two colors. Can't miss that way."

Max and Catherine avoided each other's eyes. Max stared out the window at the mare and wagon as though it were the first time he had seen them.

"Don't know why I chatter so. It just seems so . . . quiet," Edna's voice dribbled away.

Neither Max nor Catherine stepped in to fill the temporary void in the conversation, and Edna stood so fast she almost upset her chair. She jumped to the stove, slicing meat from a ham lying on a carving board. A moment later the meat was sizzling.

"I've got some eggs. I could fry up a few for you."

Catherine and Max shook their heads, and Edna busied herself at the stove, paying more attention to the ham than necessary. Zeb watched her, his head cocked to one side.

The ham was delicious, done to a fine turn as Edna had said, but Catherine just picked at the meat.

"I swear," Edna said softly. "You look like you've lost your best friend. Anything I can do?"

"Just the wind," Catherine said. "It sounds so lonesome."

"It does at that," Edna said, almost in a whisper.

"Child, the prairie is a big empty, and we try to fill it with our lives, our laughter, our children and good men like Zeb and Max. But it's so big . . . and we're so small."

Silence stretched then. Black coffee in chipped porcelain cups mesmerized the two couples.

Edna finally charged into the silence.

"Look at me," she said, "sitting around here moping when I've got news to tell."

She smiled, but her face twisted with the effort.

"Well, it seems that after the banker Phillips was found cavorting in the nude, the bank directors decided they needed to check the books.

"Found out the banker was in the till up to his elbows. At least they think it was him. They couldn't prove it was, and he couldn't prove it wasn't, so they told him to skedaddle.

"Before he left, the banker got into his cups at Millard's and made a speech. Said he was the victim of the monied interests. Said that he was too anxious to help the little man to suit the other owners of the bank. Said that he intended to do something about the travesty of justice perpetrated by those out-of-state money men who aim to suck dry the blood of Montanans.

"Right there, the banker pledged that he would run for high office in this state to uphold the interests of the little man as has always been his intent.

"That man can talk. I heard that the men in the bar were cheering by the time he hightailed it out of Prairie Rose."

"Cheers," Catherine said, lifting her cup, and the four burst into nervous laughter.

"And I've saved the best for last," Edna said, reaching into a porcelain cookie jar behind her. "The Halls stopped by yesterday, or was it the day before?" she asked, looking at Zeb.

"Well, doesn't make any difference. They had

stopped in at the Coles, and this letter was waiting for you," she said, handing it to Catherine.

Catherine took the letter as though she were receiving the sacrament. She pressed it to her face, believing it emitted the faint scent of heather.

"It's from my mother," she said.

"Well, open it, child. It's not often that anyone around here gets a letter from Ireland."

Catherine smiled at Edna. "Later, maybe. I don't get many letters. My mother doesn't have much time to write." She hesitated, then, her eyes on her coffee cup. "That's not true. My mother can't write. Father O'Malley writes them for her."

"It's nice he's there to do that," Edna said, taking Catherine's hand. "Not nearly enough priests in this country yet for all the good works that need doing." Then, she grinned around the table. "I swear. This sure turned out to be a somber bunch. Must be the fall wind."

They all agreed: It was the fall wind.

Wagon loaded, ham and bacon wrapped in an old sheet, Max and Catherine headed home. They rode in silence, Catherine fingering the letter. Max handed her his pocketknife, and she cut it open.

The letter was bad news.

Catherine's older sister, Mary, and her husband had been evicted from the little farm where his family had lived "since the blood of St. Ruth dyed the shamrocks of Aughrim."

Her eyes blurred with tears, and her mind carried her back to another black day when she was still a child.

Catherine had awakened that morning to her mother's sobbing at the window. "No, no, no. . . . No, no, no. . . ." The denials paced with her breathing. Her father was standing there too, silent but solemn as a man about to be hanged.

Catherine ran to the door and opened it. The sheriff's posse and emergency men were standing in the half light before the McBridges' home, the sheriff reading something from a document.

For two centuries, the McBridge family had lived on that land, trading their labor for food and space to live and die in. And now the sheriff was telling them that they could live there no longer, that Mr. Sullivan wanted the land for cattle and not for people.

The McBridges stood outside the home, the wife hiding beneath a shawl, hand held across her mouth; the husband sagging against the side of the whitewashed stone hut.

In a pitifully short time the family possessions, rough furniture and unmatched china, were stacked outside the hut. One emergency man carried a child, still sleeping, and laid her gently on the ground. The other children stood in a half circle around their sleeping sister, the boys' pants rolled up to their knees, the girls' dresses drab as raw dirt.

And then the lawmen began tearing down the hut, stone by stone. Mrs. McBridges wailed, the keening in her voice cutting Catherine to the soul. Keening still, she pushed her way through the lawmen and grabbed a stone. Then her husband stepped forward and grabbed one, and so did the children. They tore at the hut as though it were a living thing that needed to be put out of its misery.

Catherine slipped the letter back into the envelope and held it in her lap. Words from a Charles Kickham song she had learned as a girl came softly, painfully from her lips:

My father died—we closed his eyes
Outside our cabin door—
The landlord and the sheriff, too,
Were there the day before!
And then my loving mother,
And sisters three also,
Were forced to go, with breaking hearts,
From the glen of Aherlow!

And when she spoke, her voice was flat as North Dakota.

"I would like to have the cradle."

"Fine. I've got no use for it," Max whispered.

Catherine cried, "Oh, Max" and wrapped her arms around him. He pulled the mare to a stop and took her into his arms.

"Catherine," he said softly, "are you saying you *want* to stay?"

"Let's go home, Max." Catherine smiled. "Tell me about the house again, the one we're going to build."

And Max did. They bumped across the prairie, Catherine's head on Max's shoulder; Max telling her where the house would go. Might be, he said, that he'd put in a pond below the spring for ducks and geese and plant some cottonwoods around it.